CAPTIVATED BY THE LYON

The Lyon's Den Connected World

C.H. Admirand

© Copyright 2023 by C.H. Admirand
Text by C.H. Admirand
Cover by Dar Albert

Dragonblade Publishing, Inc. is an imprint of Kathryn Le Veque Novels, Inc.
P.O. Box 23
Moreno Valley, CA 92556
ceo@dragonbladepublishing.com

Produced in the United States of America

First Edition March 2023
Print Edition

Reproduction of any kind except where it pertains to short quotes in relation to advertising or promotion is strictly prohibited.

All Rights Reserved.

The characters and events portrayed in this book are fictitious. Any similarity to real persons, living or dead, is purely coincidental and not intended by the author.

ARE YOU SIGNED UP FOR DRAGONBLADE'S BLOG?

You'll get the latest news and information on exclusive giveaways, exclusive excerpts, coming releases, sales, free books, cover reveals and more.

Check out our complete list of authors, too!

No spam, no junk. That's a promise!

Sign Up Here

www.dragonbladepublishing.com

Dearest Reader;

Thank you for your support of a small press. At Dragonblade Publishing, we strive to bring you the highest quality Historical Romance from some of the best authors in the business. Without your support, there is no 'us', so we sincerely hope you adore these stories and find some new favorite authors along the way.

Happy Reading!

CEO, Dragonblade Publishing

Additional Dragonblade books by Author C.H. Admirand

The Duke's Guard Series
The Duke's Sword
The Duke's Protector
The Duke's Shield

The Lords of Vice Series
Mending the Duke's Pride
Avoiding the Earl's Lust
Tempering the Viscount's Envy
Redirecting the Baron's Greed
His Vow to Keep (Novella)

The Lyon's Den Series
Rescued by the Lyon
Captivated by the Lyon

Other Lyon's Den Books

Into the Lyon's Den by Jade Lee
The Scandalous Lyon by Maggi Andersen
Fed to the Lyon by Mary Lancaster
The Lyon's Lady Love by Alexa Aston
The Lyon's Laird by Hildie McQueen
The Lyon Sleeps Tonight by Elizabeth Ellen Carter
A Lyon in Her Bed by Amanda Mariel
Fall of the Lyon by Chasity Bowlin
Lyon's Prey by Anna St. Claire
Loved by the Lyon by Collette Cameron
The Lyon's Den in Winter by Whitney Blake
Kiss of the Lyon by Meara Platt
Always the Lyon Tamer by Emily E K Murdoch
To Tame the Lyon by Sky Purington
How to Steal a Lyon's Fortune by Alanna Lucas
The Lyon's Surprise by Meara Platt
A Lyon's Pride by Emily Royal
Lyon Eyes by Lynne Connolly
Tamed by the Lyon by Chasity Bowlin
Lyon Hearted by Jade Lee
The Devilish Lyon by Charlotte Wren
Lyon in the Rough by Meara Platt
Lady Luck and the Lyon by Chasity Bowlin
Rescued by the Lyon by C.H. Admirand
Pretty Little Lyon by Katherine Bone
The Courage of a Lyon by Linda Rae Sande
Pride of Lyons by Jenna Jaxon
The Lyon's Share by Cerise DeLand
The Heart of a Lyon by Anna St. Claire

Into the Lyon of Fire by Abigail Bridges
Lyon of the Highlands by Emily Royal
The Lyon's Puzzle by Sandra Sookoo
Lyon at the Altar by Lily Harlem

Dedication

For D.J. ~ Warrior Guardian Angel and KOMH

Acknowledgements

Thank you to Tara Nina ~ author extraordinaire, plot warrior, and sister-of-my-heart, for her suggestion when I confessed, "I think I have the wrong heroine…"

Thank you to Kathryn Le Veque ~ and her fabulous Dream Team at Dragonblade Publishing! My Dream Publisher is constantly finding new ways to introduce my books to new readers while allowing me to keep my voice. Actually, it isn't really *my* voice…it's the *collective* voice of my characters who keep telling me what to write, whether it follows along with my synopsis or not. LOL!

Note to Readers

I love using family names in my books. In this book, my heroine, Adelaide, is named after my great-great-aunt Adelaide—Addy—Lippincott. There have bits and pieces of my ancestors passed down to my brother, sisters, and I over the years. My sisters and I (depending on who was not speaking to whom at the time) shared the mahogany four-poster bed that belonged to Aunt Addy. It has carved pineapples on the top of the posters. It was set up in our guest bedroom until we needed to convert it to a nursery. Since then, it's been in the closet under the eaves. I'm thinking it's time to change things up, and instead of the platform bed DJ made for us before we got married, I'm going to set up Aunt Addy's bed in its place. I hope my darling Heavenly Hubby won't mind...

So, pour a cup of tea and settle into your comfy reading spot while I tell you a story...

Prologue

ADELAIDE FERNSIDE STEPPED down from the hired coach and hesitated. The hack had delivered her to the Mayfair address her sister reluctantly divulged. Addy was on a mission to save her sister, confront the gray-eyed seducer of innocents, and demand he support Lily and their unborn child!

Righteous anger guiding her, she lifted her head and walked toward the imposing town house. She drew in a calming breath and exhaled. Time to beard the dragon in his lair!

The older servant who answered the door was solicitous until a deep voice boomed from behind him, "Who are you and what do you want?"

The fierce looking, gray-haired, impeccably dressed older gentleman had to be Adam Broadbank's father...*the earl*. His anger was a living, breathing thing.

She was about to speak when he bellowed, "You're that actress!"

"You don't understand. I'm not—"

Impossibly, his voice increased in volume. "How dare you claim to carry my son's child!"

The echo of horses' hooves on the cobblestones had her stomach tying into knots. Anyone on the entire block could hear what the man shouted at her. She needed to correct this misunderstanding immediately. "It's my—"

Passersby discreetly decreased their pace. Were they listening? Had they heard the earl slandering her sister? It was unconscionable that he would degrade Lily's gift for enchanting audiences from the stage as if it were a sin, all the while insinuating she had loose morals!

How dare he make such assumptions? This was outside of enough! She had to make him listen!

"I must speak to Adam Broadbank on a matter of urgency."

The man's face paled and lost all expression. "My son is dead." He spun on his bootheel and strode back into the house. The closing of the door punctuated his proclamation.

The shock of the earl's words sliced her to the bone. *Dead?*

Unsure where to go, or what to do, she stumbled along the sidewalk. What would she tell Lily?

She had failed. Dear Lord, how could she possibly help her sister now?

Chapter One

Eighteen months later…

"Coventry and King have finally located the actress." The relief was evident on his face.

Edmund Broadbank smiled at the mention of his brother's trusted friend and fellow officer from their days in the Royal Navy. "Thank God!" A year of false leads and dead ends had finally paid off. The aid of the Duke of Wyndmere's trusted man-of-affairs, Captain Coventry, and Gavin King of the Bow Street Runners had borne fruit.

He was almost afraid to ask where they found the woman. What steps would need to be taken to approach the actress who boldly proclaimed to their father to be carrying their brother's babe, before she disappeared into the bloody woodwork?

"They are certain this time?"

"Aye." Viscount Moreland, Colin, held up the missive in his hand.

"I still don't understand how Father managed to muck this up in the first place," Edmund grumbled.

His brother's frown was fierce as he related, "King's information confirmed the woman was our elder brother's mistress. So far he has not been able to prove her claim that he fathered her child. The only fact we do have is that he did have an affair with an actress by the name of Lily Lovecote before he died."

"Without proof, how will we know if she was telling the truth? We both know at the time our father had been certain *every* woman of lesser rank and wealth was after Adam's title, and the cachet and coin that accompanied it."

Viscount Moreland's eyes narrowed. "You remember how he reacted when I married without his advice. I knew it would be a battle from the start. I did not want to resign from my position of captain in the Royal Navy. Nor did I want to assume the bloody title of viscount…but our brother's death left me little choice. I could not ignore my duty to our family any more than I could have ignored an order from the admiralty."

"You could have refused," Edmund said.

"Would you have wanted the bloody title and all the headaches that go with it?"

Edmund snorted out a laugh. "Nay! I'm grateful to you for coming home." He paused and met his brother's steady gaze. "The navy was your life for years. I know you miss it and have noted how hard your new crew…er…the staff are working to adjust to your bellowed commands."

Colin chuckled. "Gemma constantly reminds me that I need to remember I am not on the foredeck of my ship and should adjust the volume of my speech accordingly."

"Truer words, brother. I worked alongside Adam while you were at sea. While I enjoyed the physical part of his job, pitching in when needed to help his tenant farmers, I am exceedingly pleased that I was the third son."

Colin placed his hands behind his back and paced. Edmund sensed his brother must have spent more than a few hours doing the same aboard his ship.

"There was never a question that I would ignore my duty to the title and our family," Colin remarked. "Our father would never have a say in my choice of wife. His idea of what I would find acceptable in a viscountess is laughable. Could you see me spending more than five minutes with an empty-headed beauty whose every waking moment was spent worrying over which gown to wear and when she would be able to meet with her modiste to order a new one?"

"We seem to have like ideas as to what we would find acceptable in a wife," Edmund replied. "By the by, brother, how is your lovely wife?"

Colin paused in his pacing and frowned. "She was suffering from nausea upon waking but seemed to have recovered by the time I went back to see how she was feeling."

"Probably something she ate," Edmund said. "I hope you realize what a wonderful woman Gemma is. Kind to the servants, friendly to the seamen that show up now and again whenever they are in port. Tell me again, why you need to have eyes and ears on the docks?"

The viscount shook his head. "It is best that you do not know."

"I would assume they gather information for you to use in the causes you champion in the House of Lords."

"Father accepted my marriage to Gemma far quicker than I'd anticipated."

Edmund knew his brother had closed the other subject. "How could he not?" he queried. "She saved your life during that botched duel!"

Colin agreed. "I knew she loved me, but that selfless act was the proof the earl apparently needed." He waited a beat before adding, "I doubt our father will accept the word of an actress now that our brother is not here to either confirm or deny her claim."

"I cannot believe it has taken this long to locate her," Edmund said. "Did Coventry say where she has been living? They have contacts in all levels of society in London. How could she have eluded detection for so long?"

His brother frowned. "Apparently, with the aid of friends, or mayhap relatives. There are any number of places one could conceivably hide in the country."

"Now that she has been found, it is our duty to extract the truth. If she had a babe, and if it is a son," Edmund ruminated aloud, "he would be the heir to the viscountcy." His gaze met his brother's. "How would you feel about that?"

"It would bloody well be a relief!" Colin grumbled. "I have no patience for the toadying lords who require an introduction to someone or other…or need my title to back one of their causes in the House of Lords! Why is it only former members of the King's Dragoons, navy, or regiments are those trying to seek assistance for their comrades still serving the Crown?" His sigh was heavy, his expression bleak. "What I wouldn't give to feel a well-timbered deck beneath my feet as I watch my ship's sails fill with a fair wind as we plot a course out over the open water."

"You would not balk at handing over the title to Adam's heir?"

Colin slowly smiled. "If our brother were still alive, his son would be the *heir's* heir. I would never take that away from our brother's son. Though I cannot think they would have me back, I miss the time I served in His Majesty's Royal Navy. I worked hard to attain the rank of captain. The last thing I expected was to be summoned home to take over Adam's title and role of Viscount Moreland." He paused, murmuring, "I miss his acerbic wit and zest for life."

"He would always drag me with him on his trips to father's estates," Edmund remarked. "We worked side by side thatching cottages, building rock walls, digging drainage ditches—although digging in the rain was never a task I looked forward to."

"What about tedious bookkeeping and tallying of supplies?"

Edmund shrugged. "Recordkeeping and adding sums were an essential part of the duties attached to the title."

"Aye, unless you have a steward you trust implicitly handling the task for you," his brother replied. "Truth be told, I'd rather be writing in my ship's log bemoaning our dwindling stores while we wait for a supply ship than dealing with the minutiae of details required to run Templeton House or Moreland Chase."

Edmund glanced about him. "I, for one, am relieved Father has decided to stay at Moreland Chase. The Borderlands is almost far enough away to keep his meddling to a minimum."

"But not to keep him from hounding you to marry?"

Edmund did not bother to answer. He answered the question with a question. "Why do you think Father sent the woman away without speaking to her?"

His brother frowned. "He was grieving. Though why he did not demand to know where she was staying, or at least speak to the woman, I cannot fathom. What if she plans to blackmail Father?"

Edmund opened his mouth to protest, but his brother raised a hand to continue.

"Not an excuse for his treatment of the woman who could very well have been carrying the heir to the viscountcy. Our brother was the son he molded in his image. I believe he grieves for that as much as he grieves the loss of our brother."

Sorrow had Edmund's throat tightening. When would he stop seeing Adam everywhere he turned?

He cleared his throat to speak. "All was right in Father's world. His eldest son was the viscount, you excelled in the life you chose at sea serving the Crown, and I... Well, I have always been there to help with whatever task our brother asked of me." It hit him then that he'd never had a future he dreamed of chasing. "I had no desire to join the clergy, or a regiment. I always saw my life as a physical one, repairing Father's tenants' cottages, barns, and the like—I usually skipped out on the actual bookkeeping."

Colin clapped a hand to Edmund's shoulder. "I'd be more than happy to have you continuing in that role, brother...unless you prefer to start with tallying the supplies."

Edmund snorted with laughter. "Not bloody likely."

His brother admitted, "It was worth a shot."

Worry clawed at Edmund. "You believe her claim, don't you?"

"You and I both know our brother's penchant for frequenting the theatre—Covent Garden, Drury Lane, Haymarket... He preferred dallying with actresses to the barmaids."

"You were not here to see the endless parade of debutantes—the Incomparables, wallflowers, and bluestockings Father was constantly trying to tempt our brother with. Adam flatly refused to court any of them."

"If I hadn't already joined the King's Navy, I would have in order to escape Father's machinations."

Edmund felt the frustration of having but half of the information they needed building inside of him. Refusing to give in to it, he asked, "Were there any specifics in Coventry's missive?"

"King and his Bow Street Runners have been following *Mrs.* Fernside since they picked up her trail a fortnight ago."

"A false name?"

"Nay—apparently it is her maiden name."

"Anything else of note?"

"Coventry's contacts have assured him Mrs. Adelaide Fernside is the *actress* we have been searching for."

"Do you suppose our father used 'actress' as a slur, as well as a reason to turn his back and slam the door in her face?"

"You may have the right of it," Colin said. "She would not have been Father's choice, and therefore beneath his notice."

The brothers looked at one another and unconsciously assumed the same stance: shoulders back, feet spread, jaws clenched—ready for anything.

The knock on the library door had them both bracing for trouble.

The viscount nodded to his brother as he replied, "Enter."

Their butler bowed and held out a sealed note. "An urgent missive just arrived, your lordship."

"Thank you, Hanson."

"Shall I have the messenger wait for a reply?"

"If you would, please."

The butler bowed and went in search of the waiting messenger.

"Who is it from?" Edmund asked.

The viscount broke the wax seal and frowned. "Gavin King." A few moments later, he was chuckling.

His laughter had Edmund grumbling, "What in the bloody hell is so amusing?"

Colin grinned. "Apparently you are about to follow the same advice you gave me a year ago."

"What advice?"

"I believe it is time for *you* to step into the Lyon's Den, brother."

"Have you lost your mind, Colin? I have no intention of marrying!"

He handed Edmund the missive. "Read this and then tell me if you still refuse to seek Mrs. Dove-Lyon's assistance in finding a bride."

Edmund skimmed the short message and snorted with derision. King's men had traced Mrs. Fernside to Lyon's Gate Manor—home to the notorious Black Widow of Whitehall—and her establishment, the Lyon's Den. "I repeat, I have no intention of marrying."

His brother's glare almost set the kindling in the fireplace ablaze. "Would you prefer that the woman find a man of lesser means and station in life whose character is unknown to us to raise our nephew—our brother's heir?"

Edmund raked a hand through his hair and swore. "What if she refuses to accept me after the way our father treated her?"

"We must at least convince the woman of our intention to help, not harm her or her babe." Colin looked at Edmund. "The chances that the babe is Adam's outweighs your aversion to the possibility of marriage."

Edmund grunted.

When Colin did not continue to harangue him, he studied his older brother's face. Lines creased his forehead, and his visage was one of doom. His brother was not normally given to showing emotion. He must be truly worried.

"What is it?" Edmund asked.

"Coventry never fails to get whatever information he is after. We need to discover whether we have a niece or nephew." Colin cleared his throat and continued, "We cannot allow our brother's former mistress to look for another protector or husband until we hear the truth from her lips!"

"What if she truly wishes to marry?" Edmund asked. "Do we have the right to take that away from her?"

Instead of answering the question, his brother stated, "Father would never let us hear the end of it if we knew the woman sought a husband at the Lyon's Den and did nothing to stop her."

"I do not believe it is within our rights to keep her from seeking a husband."

The viscount growled, "I don't give a bloody damn if the woman wants to marry or not. We need answers! If Father were here, he'd demand them."

Colin's hands clenched into fists, and Edmund braced for the blow. His brother had a quick temper and a wicked right hook.

But the viscount's snort of laughter surprised him. "I'm not saying you should offer marriage to our brother's former mistress. I'm suggesting you seek Mrs. Dove-Lyon's assistance in looking for a bride—and a private discussion with the actress to find out what we must know!"

"I'm leery of your plan, brother," Edmund said. "What if I win whatever ridiculous wagers she comes up with and she expects me to select a bride?"

Colin grinned. "Win the wagers, but before you select a bride, insist on a private audience with the actress. Mayhap you will be able to bargain with her."

"Why in the bloody hell would the Black Widow of Whitehall agree?"

"For enough coin, I'd wager Mrs. Dove-Lyon would agree to whatever we ask. Do not forget, she has a soft spot for me."

Edmund snorted. "I believe the soft spot is in *your* head!"

His brother chuckled. "Rescuing and then competing for the honor of winning Gemma's hand in marriage changed my life. Speak to the Black Widow, bargain with her. Trust me, she will accept."

Edmund would not give his brother the satisfaction of admitting his plan would garner the information they needed, or that he may have convinced him that finding a wife as lovely as Colin's might not be such a hardship after all.

"I'm not ready to marry." Uncertainty twined with doubt, knotting in his gut. "What can I offer Mrs. Fernside to entice her to meet with you?"

"Tell her our home will be open to herself and her son, who will be raised in the lap of luxury as heir to the viscountcy."

Edmund's brow furrowed. "Have you discussed this with Gemma? Will she agree to let our brother's former mistress and his illegitimate son live with you?"

"Nay, but I will."

"What if she has a daughter?"

Colin laid a hand on his brother's shoulder. "It matters not. The offer would be the same. Look around you, Edmund—surely the woman would leap at the opportunity to live here."

"With my brother who just yesterday threatened to hang one of the footmen by the yardarms if you caught him smiling at your wife again?"

"A misjudgment on my part, as my dear wife informed me. Besides, I've not had the time to reinforce the chandelier hanging above the entryway. Best see to that before I hang anyone from it."

Edmund roared with laughter. "Tell me again how Gemma puts up with you?"

Colin's gaze lit as if from within. "The lass loves me. Find a lass of your own, Edmund. If you are as lucky as I am, she will change your life."

Edmund smiled. "You married a wonderful woman, Colin. I envy you."

"Why bother? Meet with Mrs. Dove-Lyon and make the arrangements necessary to ensure *you* will be the one to win the hand of Mrs. Fernside. Do not forget to have papers drawn up and signed by the proprietress."

"I suppose that would be necessary."

"You cannot have forgotten the underhanded way Gemma's father tried to tear my wife from my arms?" Colin's voice increased in volume when he added, "The bloody bastard claimed contracts had already been signed and the dowry handed over to Harkwell!"

"Nay, and neither will you. But Gemma is married to you...and she is safe from the Harkwells of this world."

Colin grunted.

"How does the lovely Gemma put up with your grunts and mumbles?"

Colin smiled. "She loves me."

"Aye, brother, she does."

"I didn't believe love existed," the viscount confided.

"I had my doubts until you married Gemma. 'Tis obvious you dote on the woman, and she cares for you."

"The lass loves me." Striding over to the door, the viscount opened it and bellowed, "Where's the messenger?" The footman's face paled, and Colin said, "Find him!"

Edmund chuckled. "When will you cease roaring as if you stand on the quarterdeck of your ship?"

His brother stood on the threshold of the room and turned to reply, "When I've either been consigned to the deep in Davy Jones' Locker or have cocked up my toes and shuffled off this mortal coil."

"Surprisingly eloquent of you. Although I do pity your staff until you find a more appropriate level of speaking indoors, brother."

Colin's lips twitched, but he did not smile. "They are well compensated. Ah, Hanson, thank you for bringing the messenger." Turning to the young man, he instructed, "Wait a moment while I pen my response."

"Aye, your lordship."

The viscount dipped his quill in the inkwell, wrote his reply, sanded it, folded it, and sealed it.

Colin's words would no doubt read as if he were bellowing. Though Edmund's glance at his brother had him keeping that thought to himself.

When the butler and the messenger left, Colin turned and asked, "What are you standing here for? You need to leave immediately for Lyon's Gate Manor!"

Edmund did not bother to respond as Colin strode from the room as if his ship were under attack and he was about to bellow the command to return fire!

Time was of the essence. He straightened his cuffs, buttoned his frockcoat, and asked to have the carriage brought around. He thanked Hanson and accepted his top hat and gloves from him. He was more than ready to face the Black Widow of Whitehall and gain her agreement.

Edmund would extract the information they needed from Mrs. Fernside.

Chapter Two

"Thank you for agreeing to meet with me, Mrs. Dove-Lyon."

"Your request intrigued me, Mrs. Fernside." Bessie motioned for the younger woman to be seated. When she had, the proprietress took the time to study the girl to decide if she would agree to take the young widow under her wing and find her a suitable husband.

The tea tray arrived, and the maid asked, "Would you like me to pour, Mrs. Dove-Lyon?"

"No, thank you. Would you ask Titan to ensure we have a private chat?"

"Right away." The maid scurried out of the door and closed it behind her.

"I prefer to speak to all of my potential brides without interruption." She poured their tea and passed the delicate pink and white cup and saucer to her guest, openly studying her. She was a pale English rose. Slender figure, pleasing features, honey-blonde hair, and mermaid's eyes—a fascinating shade of blue green. "I must say, you are quite lovely…such an unusual eye color. I have only seen it once before."

The young woman's hands trembled, and her fear washed over Bessie. Any number of possibilities brought young women—and their exasperated parents—to her door. Debtors' prison, accosted by a member of the *ton*, facing social ruin, a hellion or bluestocking, forced marriage... "Are you running away from a forced marriage?"

Mrs. Fernside seemed taken aback by the question, but answered readily enough. "No."

"Did a gentleman force his attentions on you? Are you with child?"

The younger woman squared her shoulders, and temper flashed in the depths of her eyes. "My sister was not forced—"

ADELAIDE CLAPPED HER hands over her mouth. She had not meant to mention Lily. She was afraid the proprietress would send her on her way, and knew she would have to divulge the truth.

"Forgive me for the deception, but I have no other way of providing for my nephew."

Mrs. Dove-Lyon placed her teacup and saucer on the table between them. "Let's start at the beginning, shall we? What is your sister's name?"

"Lily Lovecote."

"Ah, those lovely blue-green eyes of yours are distinctive, although your sister's coloring is more dramatic with her raven hair."

"You know my sister?"

"I have been to Covent Garden a time or two. She has the talent to hold an audience in the palm of her hand."

Addy smiled. "She has since we were young."

"Where is your sister now?" Addy hesitated, and Mrs. Dove-Lyon reminded her, "If you expect me to assist you, you must tell me what I need to know. Where is your sister?"

"Staying with her…er…friend."

"Having heard of her triumphant return to the stage after a life-threatening illness"—the proprietress' gaze leveled on Addy—"I take it she was pregnant and not ill."

"Yes."

"She left you responsible for the care of your nephew?"

Tears welled up, but Addy refused to let them fall. "It was my suggestion. Lily was more than happy to cart her son with her to the theatre for a time. We argued over what was best for him until the morning I woke to his cries…and the note that she was no longer able to care for him."

"I see. I take it she felt you were more suited to the role of mother than herself?"

"Don't be too quick to judge Lily. She has always been the beautiful sister, fawned over by our parents. When their carriage lost a wheel and overturned and they were killed, we were forced to leave our home by heir—our cousin."

"Where did you go? What did you do?"

"Grandmother bequeathed her home to our mother…and when she died, it went to me. I gathered what little I could and took my younger sister to live at Thorne House."

"Resourceful of you," the widow said. "Why has your sister not sought my aid? A wealthy husband would be more than able to take care of her and her babe."

Addy could not meet the older woman's veiled gaze when she admitted, "Lily reminded me a few days before she left that she intended to return to the throngs of her adoring fans. She has had offers to set her up in a lavish lifestyle."

It hurt to admit that her sister only thought of herself. Hadn't that been in part her fault? Addy had continued to feed her sister's need to be the center of attention even after their parents' death by constantly assuring Lily of her talent and beauty.

"She could not abide living in the countryside. The theatre was her life. Struggling to earn a living from the land and taking care of tenant farmers and ourselves was not."

Mrs. Dove-Lyon's voice didn't waver when she inquired, "And what of her babe?"

Love for her nephew filled Addy's heart to overflowing. "He is a beautiful babe with a sweet temperament to match. I realized if I married, it would give him a name…and a father who would love and protect him."

"Did either you or your sister attempt to contact the babe's father?"

"Lily sent a missive to him. When he did not respond, I traveled to London—once Lily confided in me who'd fathered her child. The earl slandered my sister at the top of his lungs on the sidewalk outside their home in Mayfair." She shivered, remembering the anger in the older man's voice. "He refused to listen or grant me the opportunity to speak with him."

Mrs. Dove-Lyon freshened both of their cups. "Drink while it is still warm." Adelaide did as she was told while the proprietress continued, "As with most who are titled, they think of the possibility of scandal first, the needs of others second. Did you find out anything else of import?"

A lone tear sneaked past Addy's guard. "Adam Broadbank was dead."

Mrs. Dove-Lyon paused with her cup to her lips. She set it on the saucer then slowly lowered it to the table between them. "I recall Viscount Moreland succumbing to a virulent fever last year."

Adelaide trembled. "I didn't realize my sister's lover was a viscount, though it wouldn't have mattered if he was titled. Lily was beside herself, believing he had abandoned her in her time of need. Though at first she insisted he bored her, and she had shown him the door."

The older woman listened intently before saying, "Earl Templeton is not one to suffer fools. To be honest, the man is a bit of a prig."

Adelaide heartily agreed. "He was rude, insufferable, and bellowed that my sister was all but a liar while carriages rumbled past his town house."

"How have you managed to hide all these months?"

"Hide?"

"I have it on good authority that Broadbank's brothers, Colin—the new Viscount Moreland—and Edmund have been trying to find you."

Surprise flitted across Addy's features before she asked, "Why in Heaven's name would they be looking for me?"

Mrs. Dove-Lyon chuckled. "There are those who apparently have you confused with your sister and believe *you* to be the actress who had the affair with Viscount Moreland."

"But I look nothing like my sister," she protested.

"Now that I have met you, I can assure you the resemblance is quite remarkable, with the exception of your hair color. Actresses have been known to don wigs for different roles, so those searching for you must have been concentrating on other physical aspects. Your slender figure, your height, the shape of your face...and the distinct shade of your mermaid's eyes."

"Whoever they are, they must be mad to think we look alike. Lily is the beautiful one, not me."

"I know two of the men searching for you by name and reputation—neither of them are in a position to make mistakes."

"Well, they have this time!" Addy insisted.

"Let us agree to disagree. Rumors are often founded on a sliver of fact. As I make it my business to confirm such rumors, I am merely telling you what I have observed. The resemblance is uncanny."

"Why would you need to confirm rumors that are patently false?"

"In my business, it would not do to discover one of the young ladies seeking my help to secure a husband is already wed."

"I should say not!" Addy said.

"Do you believe in fate?" Adelaide was still reeling from the fact that the Broadbank brothers had been searching for Lily—er...her, when Mrs. Dove-Lyon advised, "I was instrumental in finding the perfect match for the viscount, although he was new to the title at the time and preferred to be referred to by his position with the Royal Navy—Captain Broadbank." She frowned. "I admire the man and cannot imagine that he would not come to your aid.

"Unfounded rumors were circulating about the viscount's death, and then again when Captain Broadbank returned to accept the mantle of viscount. I, myself, have been a widow for a number of years. Though your sister did not marry the viscount, I am deeply sorry for her loss."

Bottled-up emotions bubbled to the surface, and fear that the situation was spiraling out of control had tears threatening. Striving to keep them from falling, Adelaide fumbled with her reticule, trying to find her handkerchief. When a lace-edged bit of linen was handed to her, she gratefully accepted it. "Forgive me. Do you think Adam's brothers will try to take my nephew from me?"

"I would guess since they are looking for you, they believe you are your sister and may wish to discuss something of import with you." When Addy did not answer right away, the proprietress added, "You do realize, as Adam Broadbank's heir, your nephew is by right Viscount Moreland."

"I will never willingly give the child away...to anyone...for any reason."

"You have admitted he is your nephew. Have you considered what kind of life could be his as the heir?"

"My sister knows I would not give my nephew up."

"Not even if he was acknowledged by the earl?"

"Not even then," Adelaide replied.

"Excellent. You are not willing to give up, and you appear to be willing to fight for your nephew."

"To my last breath."

The proprietress narrowed her eyes at Adelaide. "Mayhap you would prefer to wait until you meet with the viscount and his brother before we come to an agreement."

Addy shook her head. "I am running out of funds and cannot impose upon the elderly staff remaining at Thorne House to take care of us without compensation."

"There are no cousins or relatives who could take you in?"

"No one, as my cousin has cut us off after he claimed his inheritance." Addy paused. "Would a small estate in great need of repair be a detriment to finding a husband?"

"Not at all. I'm merely questioning you to ensure I have all of the facts pertinent to your situation."

"I understand. If the viscount and his brother still wish to meet with me, I'd prefer it to happen once I have secured the protection of the man I am to marry."

"I will see what I can do, although I cannot imagine the viscount, or his brother, would approve."

"It is not their place to approve or disapprove of what I do." When Mrs. Dove-Lyon did not immediately respond, Adelaide studied the veiled woman before adding, "Mayhap now you understand why I present myself as a widow, though I use my maiden name."

"A young woman in your unusual position must make decisions that others would question. I admire your spirit, my dear. A word of caution: it may be a bit difficult to explain to your husband-to-be, but I would tell him the truth—all of it."

The tension in her stomach eased as her worst fear was resolved—the Black Widow of Whitehall would not turn her away. "Do you have anyone in mind?"

"I have a number of gentlemen in mind."

"How do you choose?"

The woman's bold laughter had Adelaide wondering if the rumors she had heard about the Lyon's Den were founded on fact.

"You can expect to hear from me—" The loud knock on the door interrupted their conversation and seemed to irritate the hostess. She ignored the knock. "As I was saying—"

The door opened, and a man beckoned to her.

"Titan! I told you I was not to be disturbed."

"'Tis urgent."

"Very well. Titan, would you kindly show Mrs. Fernside to the ladies' observation gallery?"

"Of course." He bowed and motioned with his hand for Adelaide to precede him.

She noted more than a few gentlemen's heads turning as they walked through the establishment. She ignored them and followed Titan around the perimeter of the main gambling room and to the far corner at the back of the room.

"The stairs are this way."

They ascended, and she was shown into a room with large windows along one wall.

"One of the maids will be happy to answer any questions you might have. Mrs. Dove-Lyon has rules that must be followed."

"I do not plan to break any rules," Addy replied.

"See that you do not. You may observe the eligible men gathered in the gaming room below until your allotted time is over. I shall come for you then to escort you to a carriage that will take you wherever you wish to go."

"Thank you."

He paused in front of the door. "Do not bang on the glass."

"Why would…?"

Her voice trailed off as he opened the door and slipped out of the room.

The longer she was in the Lyon's Den, the more she questioned whether her decision to seek out Mrs. Dove-Lyon had been prudent.

Chapter Three

"Oh, he is quite handsome, don't you think?"

Addy turned toward the soft voice and could not help but smile at the rapt expression on the younger woman's face. She was dressed in the latest fashion, a lovely confection in the palest of rose, accenting the young woman's peaches-and-cream complexion, wavy, dark hair and warm brown eyes.

Addy cleared her throat and asked, "Which one?"

The young woman surprised her by slipping her arm through Adelaide's. "Across the room by the doors leading to the gardens."

Adelaide shifted her gaze toward the doors and squinted to see. "The tall man with the ink-black hair or the one speaking to him?"

"Not the tall gentleman. He appears to have eaten too many sour grapes. The other one with the fiery hair and broad smile."

At that moment, both gentlemen turned and looked up.

"Can they see us through the glass?" Addy asked.

"Yes, and we can see them."

Worry had her belly churning. "Will we have any say at all?"

The young woman lifted one shoulder and let it fall. "I am not quite certain. Though Mrs. Dove-Lyon has made wonderful matches for two of my very good friends."

"I have only just heard of this establishment. Although we had a meeting, I am still unsure of which gentlemen she has in mind for me." When the other woman remained silent, Addy realized she'd forgotten her manners. "How unkind of me not to introduce myself, my name is Mrs. Fernside…er, Adelaide."

The woman's smile lit up the entire room. "Catherine…Lady Catherine Huntington. My friends all call me Kit."

"Isn't that a nickname for Christopher?"

The lilting laughter filled the room and eased a bit of Adelaide's worry. "Aye. You must call me Kit. Shall I call you Adelaide or Addy?"

"Addy." The rest of her worries slipped away as she allowed herself to be drawn in by the woman's friendly candor. "Surely we cannot be so informal on such short acquaintance, can we?"

Kit tossed her head, and one chestnut curl sprang free from its pins. "I do not give a fig! Father has thrown up his hands and refuses to speak to me." Leaning closer, she rasped, "He has no idea my aunt has brought me here."

Recalling her own ill treatment at the hands of Earl Templeton, Adam's father, Addy asked, "What will he do when he finds out?"

"What can he do? I shall be married by morning."

"Oh dear, that soon? I did not realize. Mrs. Dove-Lyon only mentioned finding the perfect match for me."

"It is not the same for everyone. It depends on the…er…circumstances. As you are a widow, mayhap you are not in as much of a hurry as some of the rest of us."

"How so?"

"You've heard of the Season's Incomparables?"

Adelaide smiled. "Of course."

"There are those of us who are the *Unmarriageables*."

Though not a member of the *ton*, Adelaide was well aware of the Season—its reigning beauties, wallflowers, and bluestockings. "But you are so lovely and have such a sparkling personality. How could you be unmarriageable?"

"I loathe staying indoors and plying a needle and thread for hours on end. Don't bother to ask me to speak of the latest fashions—I'd much rather discuss what is happening in the House of Lords." Kit grinned. "I prefer spending my time in the stables taking care of Father's horses and sneaking out to ride them whenever his back is turned."

Adelaide wondered what she had been thinking seeking help here. She was not of the quality...and did not belong. "I am not from the same social level as you, Kit."

"You are a widow of some means, or Mrs. Dove-Lyon would never have taken you on."

"Do you know, I've never been befriended by a member of the *ton*. I have been shunned by them—"

"As have I," Kit confided. "Those empty-headed leeches have nothing to recommend them beyond their face and form. After their fathers secure a match that will increase their own pockets and elevate their daughters in society, those poor girls will be bundled off to country estates, where they will be nothing more than broodmares. God help them if they cannot produce an heir!"

Compared to what Adelaide had experienced, it sounded so very bleak a future. "You have a very cynical view of society." When Kit shrugged, Adelaide pulled her closer to her side. "I'm sorry not to have met you before today. I would have enjoyed getting to know you."

Kit sighed. "I shall speak to Mrs. Dove-Lyon. I have paid her an exorbitant amount of coin—the very least she could do besides matching me with that auburn-haired god is to give me your address. We shall write to one another and keep in touch."

Adelaide was humbled by Kit's offer. "I should like that above all things."

"Oh look! Mrs. Dove-Lyon is speaking to three men. Over there, by the door to her office." The two women studied the men from their vantage point.

"What do you think their story is?" Adelaide asked. "Are these gentlemen in want of a wife that desperately?"

"Most are, but again, their reasons differ." Kit poked her in the side. "Smile!"

Adelaide laughed. "Whatever for?"

"They are looking this way."

Unease swept up from her toes. Could she do this? Marry a man she did not know—or care for? She'd never even had a beau…there simply hadn't been time with raising Lily on her own.

Just as quickly as the men glanced up, they turned back around, nodding at Mrs. Dove-Lyon.

The door opened, and Titan motioned to Addy. "Mrs. Fernside. Your carriage awaits."

Adelaide hugged Kit. "If you write, I shall answer, though I cannot make any promises, as my future is bleak and unknown."

"Take heart and trust that Mrs. Dove-Lyon will come through for us."

They were smiling as they parted.

THE DOOR OPENED, and Edmund smiled. "Mrs. Dove-Lyon. You are looking well."

"Mr. Broadbank, what brings you to my establishment?"

He gathered from her tone that she had been disturbed. "I beg your pardon. Have I interrupted?"

She waved a hand in front of her. "I am quite adept at juggling appointments, Mr. Broadbank. You were about to tell me what brings you to my establishment."

"The usual reasons—however, it is quite urgent that we speak."

"I doubt it has to do with your brother. I only have success where my matches are concerned."

He chuckled. "Colin and Gemma are deliriously happy."

She inclined her head. "I trust matters regarding the despicable Harkwell, and her unfortunate father, have been settled."

He frowned at her. "Aye, though a situation has developed, and I find myself in need of a wife."

When she didn't immediately respond, he wished she would take off that ridiculous veil so he could see what the woman was thinking. He was at a distinct disadvantage not being able to see her expression.

"Immediately?" she asked.

"Is that a problem?"

"Not at all. Won't you sit down? I have another matter to settle before we speak. I shall be right back."

He grudgingly sat on the oversized wing-backed chair. It could fit two quite comfortably. His thoughts strayed to just how comfortably before he shook his head. *No point in going there any longer. Once you marry, you shall not be visiting your favorite barmaid at the inn.*

The door opened, and Mrs. Dove-Lyon bustled back into the room. "Now then. We can speak uninterrupted. What did you have in mind for a bride?"

"I understand a young woman—an actress—was seen entering your establishment. I will pay whatever price, but I must implore you not to make a match for her until I have spoken to her."

Unmoved by his statement, she asked, "What possible interest could you have in an actress—aside from the usual ones?"

"I have something of import to discuss with her."

"Such as?"

He did not want to blurt out the reasons, but he must use everything in his arsenal to convince the difficult woman to agree. "Colin and I have been searching for her for well over a year. She was our brother's mistress and rumored to be carrying his babe—if she delivered a boy, he is the true heir to the viscountcy!"

"Shouldn't the viscount be the one to speak with me?"

Edmund snorted with laughter. "Need I remind you he is married? I doubt his wife would approve of his meeting with you."

"Mayhap he would not be averse to setting his wife aside, if he would be able to retain the viscountcy by marrying the mother of your eldest brother's babe?"

Edmund shot to his feet. "That is contemptible!"

"Precisely, and the response I hoped to hear. Now let us get down to my terms, shall we?"

"You agree not to search for a match for her until I have spoken with her and discover whether or not she bore Adam a son?" Edmund asked.

"What if she bore your brother a daughter?"

"Either way, it is imperative that I speak with her."

"Do you wish to wed her?"

"Good God, no!"

Mrs. Dove-Lyon watched him intently. "If you consent to three wagers, win them, and offer a sum I could not refuse, I shall arrange for you to speak with her—privately."

"I know you are a woman of your word," he replied. "Agreed."

"Excellent. Now then, Mr. Broadbank, shall we discuss my fee?"

Chapter Four

ADELAIDE KEPT LOOKING over her shoulder as she rushed along the sidewalk to the waiting hansom cab. Mrs. Dove-Lyon had not been what she expected. Nor had meeting Lady Catherine—Kit—and forming a fast friendship with her.

Smiling to herself, she reasoned that her life had indeed turned a corner—this time in a direction that would lead to what she hoped to provide for her darling nephew and his future.

Lily had indulged in more than one whirlwind romance in the last few years, while Addy had been the one at home trying to scrape together enough coin to keep a roof over their heads and help their tenant farmers. They depended upon one another. It was a delicate circle. If broken, and the farmers had not seed to plant, or sharpened plows with which to till the soil, she would not earn the revenues that she poured back into the estate and the farmers. She wished there was enough left over to pay the back wages she owed to their loyal pensioners.

The carriage wheel struck a rut between two cobblestones and jarred her back to the present. She had never thought to have a gentleman court her…how could she skip that part and jump straight into marriage?

Hand to her throat, she rasped aloud, "What have I done?"

Taken the next step toward securing a future for the babe who depends on you.

Was she doing the right thing? Would marriage to a total stranger secure the necessary protection the true heir to the Moreland Viscountcy required? She would not feel safe unless she had a strong man by her side. Her nephew deserved no less.

She would do everything in her power to protect her nephew from the harsh reality and cruel, wagging tongues of the *ton*. As she had no means of entrée into society, since the earl had turned his back on her sister—and herself—she had to rely on Mrs. Dove-Lyon and her establishment to secure a suitable husband.

Adelaide prayed she was making the right choice.

As she stepped down from the carriage, she thought only of her nephew and the opportunities she would now be able to offer him. Rushing into the alleyway, she entered the building and ascended the stairs. Her hand was poised to knock, but the door swung open before she could.

"There you are, Mrs. Fernside. Someone just woke up from his nap and is waiting for you."

Miss Wythe greeted her the same way every time she opened the door. Addy felt blessed that one of the pensioners, Mr. Wythe, had written to his sister, who agreed to let Addy and her nephew stay with her while in London. She felt welcome. *Wanted*.

After pressing a kiss to the little one's cheek, she asked, "Was Adam a good babe for you while I was gone?"

"He is an angel."

Addy laughed. "Even I know how quickly he can go from sitting quietly and banging a spoon on pots and pans to running from you to avoid taking a nap."

Miss Wythe shook her head. "He hasn't tried to run away from me—yet."

"What I would do without your help, Miss Wythe?"

"Now, now. I told you to call me Nora."

"I don't want to appear disrespectful. After all you, your brother, and his wife have done for us, opening Thorne House to us and staying on even though I have been unable to pay them their back wages. How can I possibly repay you?"

"By finding the right man to marry. You need a strong man by your side. These are troubling times for you and your nephew. You've taken on a heavy burden raising him when his mother is off..." Nora sighed. "Forgive me. It is not my place to judge another. You need a strong man standing beside you to protect you and the little one from those who would seek to take advantage of you."

"I think I do," Addy confided. "I have just learned Adam's uncles have been searching for him and his mother. For some odd reason, they have been led to believe *I* am his mother."

"Trust no one. I have heard unsavory things, but I will not gainsay my brother. If he felt the choice you are making is the correct one for a woman in your situation, then who am I to quibble?" Nora raised her chin. "Watch your back, Mrs. Fernside."

"I shall. I promise."

The older woman nodded. "I have the kettle on. Why don't you take this little one and spend some time with him while I brew a pot of tea? I baked a lovely teacake while he was sleeping."

Addy cuddled her nephew close, and when he wrapped his chubby little arms around her neck and laid his head on her shoulder, she finally relaxed. Would the gentleman Mrs. Dove-Lyon selected be as accepting of her nephew as she had been when her sister abandoned him? She would put the question to the faceless gentleman she hoped would be the answer to their situation.

As quickly as the little one settled in her arms, he was soon squirming to be put down. With a sigh, she realized he was no longer satisfied with being held and cuddled. He needed to explore his surroundings—all the while testing her patience with his penchant for ignoring her when she told him no.

"Let us see if we can tempt him with a bit of cake and a sip of milk," Nora suggested.

Willing to see how her nephew would react to the treat, when she sensed he would rather explore, she accepted the plate with the sliver of cake on it and broke it into small pieces.

"Adam, would you like to try some cake?"

His gray eyes widened as he stared at the bite of cake she held out to him. He toddled over to her, his steps stronger and surer every day. He placed one hand on her knee and held the other one out for the sweet treat.

"Chew it well, my love," Addy instructed. He surprised her by climbing onto her lap and sitting still while she offered him one bite at a time with sips of milk from his cup.

"He is such a good little boy," Nora commented.

"I am wondering when he will start to string more than a few words together. So far he watches and listens when I talk to him, but he appears to be a deep thinker."

"I wouldn't worry overmuch. Adam will say more when he's ready."

They chatted over tea and cake. With the warmth of her nephew in her arms, Addy was finally able to let go of her worries and enjoy the quiet moment. It would be the last one she had for quite some time—if Mrs. Dove-Lyon's prediction came true, she would be saying her vows tomorrow afternoon!

Chapter Five

EDMUND STEPPED DOWN from the hired hack and waited until it drove off before entering the alley alongside Lyon's Gate Manor. He nodded to Hermia and Helena stationed at the ladies' entry. They noted he was headed to the rear of the building but did not attempt to stop him.

Had Mrs. Dove-Lyon advised he would be arriving this evening and anticipated he would use the rear entrance? He shook his head at the thought. "I have far more to worry about than which bloody entry to use."

"Talking to yourself?"

Edmund looked up and grinned at the man stationed at the rear entry. "Snug!"

"Aye." The guard squinted and recognition crossed his features. "Broadbank, what brings you back to our door?"

"I've come back for another tot of rum."

The former military man grinned and patted his waistcoat pocket. "Just refilled my flask. Care for a sip before you enter the Lyon's Den?"

Edmund shook his head. "Not if I'm to win three wagers tonight."

Snug glanced about him, then motioned Edmund closer. "Though it may cost me my job, I heard a rumor that you will not be competing against gentlemen vying for the hand of your lady."

"Oh?" Edmund's gut roiled. "What else did you hear?"

"Your opponents in fencing and pugilism are more than they appear to be."

He clamped his jaw shut, ruminating over the news. "Experts?"

Snug shrugged.

"Thank you for the warning, my friend."

"How fares the captain and his lovely bride?"

Edmund grinned. "Happiest I have seen my brother since he was forced to become a landlubber."

Snug agreed, saying, "As it should be with the right woman." He stared at Edmund before lifting his chin toward the door. "I've heard Mrs. Dove-Lyon has chosen a lovely slip of a lass for you. Treat her kindly, respect her, and you'll receive kindness and respect in return."

"I have a meeting to attend before I compete for anyone's hand."

Snug narrowed his eyes. "Heard about that, too. I don't normally interfere, but Titan and I have taken a liking to you. There is more at play than you know."

"How so?"

The guard glanced about him before leaning close to confide, "The woman you will be meeting is not the babe's mother."

"I have it on excellent authority—"

"Keep an open mind, Broadbank. It will serve you well."

Edmund thanked the wolf standing guard at the back entry and entered the darkened hallway. Confident he would win whatever wagers the Black Widow of Whitehall challenged him to, he strode toward the light and loud voices.

"Broadbank?"

He glanced at the man walking toward him and smiled. "Titan. Good to see you."

Mrs. Dove-Lyon's head wolf and manager acknowledged the

greeting, and said, "Surprised your brother did not accompany you."

Edmund lowered his voice and said, "Keeping a low profile now that he's wed."

"The captain's a wise man."

A movement above distracted him. He glanced up and stared. "What in the bloody hell...are those ropes?"

Titan's gaze held no hint of emotion. "Are you ready for the first wager?"

Edmund looked at the height of the ceiling and the ropes waiting to be uncoiled. Turning his head, he stared at the former soldier injured in the name of the Crown. "Is it against the rules to introduce me to my rivals?"

Titan's lips twitched. "Normally it is part of our instructions—however, not in this instance."

"How many will there be?"

"Three."

"What do you know about them? Corinthians? Pinks of the *ton*? Rakehells?"

The man stared at the entrance to the smoking room. "There's one of your opponents now."

Edmund studied the man walking toward them. The fellow's confident stride and the way he carried himself spoke of time spent on horseback either hunting or for pleasure. A sportsman.

"Corinthian," Edmund said.

"Aye. A devil on horseback—wouldn't wager against him if a horse was involved."

"Noted."

"Quinton," Titan said before turning back to Edmund. "Broadbank. You'll be competing against Berges and Colgate."

"When do we meet the others?" Edmund asked.

"As only one of you will be moving on to the next wager, only the winner will advance to the next round."

"I'm ready," Quinton announced. "What's the wager?"

"Look up." Titan nodded to one of the men. Two ropes uncoiled.

"Bloody hell." The color leached from the man's face.

"Problem, Quinton?" Titan asked. It was patently obvious the man had an issue with heights.

Quinton clenched his jaw, then relaxed it. "Not at all. Shall we?"

A few of the other wolves stationed about the main gambling floor ushered those in the room to stand around the perimeter. Money changed hands, and Edmund wondered if his years spent climbing trees at Moreland Chase and scaling ladders to replace thatching would be in his favor. He shrugged out of his frockcoat, laid it across the back of a chair, and proceeded to unbutton his waistcoat before tossing it on top of his coat.

While Quinton did the same, Edmund rolled up his sleeves. He wanted as little resistance as possible when he started to climb.

The cheering started the moment he reached for the rope dangling above his head. Hand over hand he steadily pulled himself up. He felt the first blister form and break.

"Bugger it."

He was on a mission to save his niece or nephew. He kept climbing.

The cheers and jeers of those gathered did not distract him from the end goal—reaching the top of the rope before Quinton. The bloody ceiling was a good twenty feet high. Shoving that thought from his mind, he continued to climb, ignoring the burning sensation as he grasped the rope with his abused palms, pulling himself ever closer to the top.

Quinton had made it three-quarters of the way to the top when Broadbank slapped his hand to the ceiling, not surprised to see the smear of blood left behind.

Titan called out, "Broadbank will advance to the next wager."

Edmund immediately began his descent, wishing someone had

tossed him a pair of gloves at the start. His shoulders ached, but he kept going. He had two more wagers to win.

Letting go of the rope a few feet from the floor, he landed next to Titan.

"You have a quarter of an hour before your next wager," the man informed him. "Snug will see to your hands. You'll need to wrap them before the next challenge."

"Broadbank?"

Edmund turned at the sound of his name.

"Well done," Quinton said.

"If the wager had been different, you would have won."

The other man frowned at him. "How so?"

Edmund replied in a low voice, "If the wager acknowledged a man battling his fear of heights to climb that bloody rope, you would have won."

Quinton's eyes widened. "It showed?"

"Only to someone who knows the signs. Well done, Quinton."

As instructed, Edmund retreated to the rear of the building and sought out Snug, who was ready with a basin, salve, and clean strips of linen. The older man shook his head when he saw the state of Edmund's hands. "Takes a bit of time before the blisters form calluses."

Edmund winced as his hands were carefully dried and healing salve was applied. "Once Colin joined the navy, he did not return home often. Knowing my brother, he would never have admitted to ripped and bleeding hands while he learned to master the ropes."

"No seaman worth his salt would. Your brother is one of the best."

Edmund watched Snug tie off both bandages. "A good man to have at your back."

"Heed my word and keep an open mind during your meeting, and remember, all is not as it seems. You've nothing to fear here, Broadbank," Snug assured him as he offered his flask. "A bit of rum should take the sting out of your palms."

Edmund chuckled. "If I remember my brother's reaction, what you carry around in your flask would damage the lining of my stomach." Snug's raspy laughter brought a grin to his face. "Thank you, Snug—for taking care of my hands and the offer to share your rum."

"I've only ever shared my libations with one other man."

"Colin?"

"Aye, the captain."

"In that case, I'm honored and have changed my mind."

Snug grinned. "Thought you might." He handed the flask to Edmund, who took a swig. His eyes watered. After swallowing, he drew in a breath, cleared his throat, and rasped his thanks. Snug chuckled. "You'll be back to see me after this next wager. Best hurry. If you're late, you forfeit!"

"Bloody hell!" Edmund nearly collided with Titan as he rushed away.

The man glanced at Edmund's bandaged hands and motioned for him to follow. "Your next wager will be in the gardens."

"Does it involve digging?"

Titan snickered. "Nay."

Edmund followed as they threaded through the crowded gambling room. Those who'd paused to watch two men competing in a rope climb earlier were back at the tables, wagering exorbitant amounts of coin.

"Ah, Berges," Titan said to the man waiting in the doorway to the gardens. "Broadbank, you and Berges will cross swords."

"I beg your pardon?" Edmund asked.

"Only a commoner would not have learned the art of fencing," Berges remarked.

Edmund immediately took exception to the slight, but hid his reaction, merely staring at the man.

"This way, *gentlemen*," Titan said.

They followed the winding path, which led to a large, round wooden platform surrounded by meticulously clipped boxwoods. Two men, holding foils, stood waiting for them.

Titan nodded to the men and told Edmund and Berges, "Gentlemen, here are the rules."

"Rules?" Berges spat. "I was not informed of any rules."

"The rules are inflexible. Anyone who does not follow them will be disqualified."

Edmund wondered at the other man's ire, but remained silent, waiting for Titan to continue.

"This is not a duel. This is an exercise in finesse. Three touches to the torso are all that is required. Slashes drawing blood will not be permitted."

"This is not a true fencing bout," Berges barked. "A true bout—"

"Mrs. Dove-Lyon is well aware and has dictated the rules. Follow them or leave. The choice is yours."

Edmund was no stranger to holding a foil in his hand. He never won when crossing foils with his brother, but he gave as good as he got. Accepting the blade, he whipped it through the air in front of him, getting the feel of the foil and its weight. "Good balance," he murmured.

Titan asked, "Ready?"

Broadbank answered, "Yes." The other man nodded at the same time.

The men faced one another. When Titan bade them to start, they circled, parried, and riposted. Edmund saw an opening, lunged forward, and scored the first touch.

Berges' face mottled red with anger. They resumed, and this time, Berges was the one to land a touch.

Edmund's hands ached, and he knew he wouldn't be able to wield his weapon with any amount of skill for much longer. He feinted to the left, then lunged and scored a touch. Berges' erratic footwork and slashes that followed were evidence of the man's anger. Anger would not win the match. Finesse would.

Edmund saw his opening and took it, scoring a third touch. Satisfaction filled him as he backed away from his opponent and turned to hand off his weapon.

He realized his mistake when he felt the bite of the blade in his upper arm.

Berges smiled. "My foot slipped. Forgive me."

Incensed, Edmund stepped forward, fists raised. "Bloody coward!"

Before he could land a blow, Titan was standing in front of him. "You have just forfeited your right to compete in any further wagers in the Lyon's Den, Berges."

"We shall see about that!" the other man roared, rushing toward Titan, and slashing the blade toward his face.

Instinct had Edmund yanking Titan out of the way before he was skewered. Four men rushed into the garden. They relieved Berges of his weapon and formed a guard around him, escorting him from the garden and the premises.

Edmund searched Titan's closed expression before finally inquiring, "Why didn't you move out of the way?"

Titan drew in a deep breath and exhaled.

"You could have lost an eye!"

The other man shrugged, and the look in his eyes and rigid posture had Edmund recalling Colin having a similar reaction. It was during a recent violent thunderstorm. Titan—like Colin—must have been swept back in time in the middle of a battle in his thoughts.

"War is hell," Edmund murmured.

"Aye. Thank you."

"You're welcome."

"One more wager, though I've been instructed ahead of time to allow you a bit longer before you meet with your opponent if I see fit."

Titan glanced at Broadbank's arm. "You may need threads to close that slash."

Edmund's stomach flipped over. He hated needles. "Wrap it tight. It'll be fine."

"Snug's the man who sees to any injuries. Follow me."

Soon, Edmund again found himself standing before the seaman. "Berges won't be permitted entrance again," Snug muttered as he tended to the wound. "It probably burns like hell, but it is not deep."

Edmund released the breath he was holding.

"Worried?"

"Hate needles."

"Once ye've been sewn back together half a dozen times, it won't bother you as much."

"Half a dozen?" Edmund rasped.

Snug shrugged as he wound a length of linen around Edmund's upper arm. He tied it off and helped him don his bloodstained cambric shirt. "Not sure if this will last through your last wager."

"Oh?" Edmund waited for Snug to confide more, but the man must have realized he had said enough.

"Best head back. Titan will be waiting for you. Your last wager will be held in one of the private rooms near the musicians."

"Thank you for wrapping my arm."

Snug gave a brief nod before returning to his post.

Edmund's arm ached and his hands burned. Hell of a night so far. Returning to the main room, he wondered what the last wager would entail. He hoped it involved brandy—unlike his brother, Edmund enjoyed a good brandy.

Chapter Six

"Edmund Broadbank to see you."

Mrs. Dove-Lyon looked up from her correspondence and rose from her seat. "Send him in, Titan."

The wry look on her head wolf's face had her wondering what amused him as he stepped to the side to admit Broadbank. With Titan it could be anything from one of the other wagers currently in progress, to a conversation he'd overheard. She was accustomed to the unexpected and rather enjoyed their discussions.

She inwardly winced. It was best not to show emotion while dealing with those involved in a wager for the hand of one of the ladies who sought her aid. Her reputation depended on her impartiality.

Edmund Broadbank stepped over the threshold as if he were dressed to the nines…though from his bedraggled, bruised, and bloody appearance, he looked as if he'd gone three rounds with Gentleman Jackson and lost a fencing bout against Henry Angelo!

She noted the blood-soaked bandage on his arm and fought to control her anger. It was obvious Berges had ignored her ironclad rules. "Titan?"

The wolf paused with his hand to the door. "Aye?"

"I trust you have taken care of Berges?"

His steely gaze met hers. They would speak of it later. For now, she would have to be satisfied that Titan had escorted the man from her establishment.

"I have."

She inclined her head. "Send someone to relieve Snug and ask him to bring his supplies. We cannot let Mr. Broadbank leave in this condition."

"At once."

Curiously, Edmund had listened to the conversation without adding to it. Had he suffered from more than one blow to his head?

"Did Colgate knock you out?" she asked.

Broadbank's snort of derision had her lips lifting in a smile, though she knew he could not see it through the veil covering her face. "Not bloody likely."

She slipped her arm through his and gave it a tug to get him to follow her. "Please sit down before you fall down."

Surprisingly, he did as she bade him. A glance at his hands had her heart squeezing. She had not thought about the abuse the men would suffer climbing the rope. It had been suggested by Snug as a feat of skill and strength, pulling one's weight up by one's arms, and she had readily agreed. Next time, she would remember to ask for more particulars.

The knock on the door interrupted her thoughts. "Come in."

Snug carried in a large tray, set it down on her desk, and glanced at Edmund. "I see Broadbank proved himself worthy."

"Should I send for the physician?"

"Let me take another look at his arm." Turning to Edmund, he said, "Colgate seemed sure of himself."

Edmund narrowed his eyes at Snug. "A Broadbank never gives up. We go down fighting!"

"Do you mind if I speak with you, while Snug inspects your arm?"

Bessie asked. "I am concerned that the wound could have been torn open or widened."

EDMUND WISHED HE could see the woman's face and recalled his brother mentioning the same after dealing with the veiled proprietress. "I'm sure it was just the impact of the blows. A fresh bandage, wrapped tight, is all it requires."

"Let Snug tend to your arm and your other injuries." The woman did not appear ready to leave, and her next words confirmed it. "He will let us know if anything further is required."

If she was not embarrassed by his removing his tattered shirt, then he would not show his surprise that she remained in the room with him half-clothed. He had not wagered for *her* hand.

Snug helped him take off his shirt. To distract himself from the pain, Edmund asked, "Do you often have to deal with those who would cheat to win a wager?"

Mrs. Dove-Lyon drew in a breath and slowly exhaled. "More than I care to discuss. Berges has been dealt with. Do you have any complaints about your other opponents?"

"No complaints, but I would like to commend Quinton's bravery."

She tilted her head. "He only made it three-quarters of the way up the rope. How was that brave?"

"Did you know the man is afraid of heights?"

Her silence was his answer—she knew. It reminded him of the brandy wager his brother had faced—Colin could barely hold a mouthful without the urge to hurl it back. Mrs. Dove-Lyon was well informed.

Snug cleaned the slash on his arm a second time and studied the wound for longer than Edmund thought necessary. "Something wrong?" he asked.

"Aye. It appears as if Colgate managed to connect a number of blows to one spot. See where the slash is the same width here, but wider and ragged here?"

"Felt it," Edmund grumbled. "Don't need to see it."

"It'll require threads."

Edmund shot to his feet. "I believe I should take my leave."

"Sit down, Broadbank!"

The sharp command from the woman poking him in the shoulder irritated him to no end. "I'll not subject myself to a needle and thread unless it's absolutely necessary."

Snug let go of the wad of linen he had been using to press against the wound and watched as Edmund felt his face lose every ounce of color.

He cleared his throat, watching the crimson flowing from the slash onto the cloth beneath his elbow. "Apologies, Snug. Please, continue."

"Sometimes 'tis best to let it bleed a bit," Snug remarked. "You'll be right as rain once I sew it closed for you."

"Thank you for taking care of Mr. Broadbank, Snug," Mrs. Dove-Lyon said. "We cannot have him calling upon Mrs. Fernside in such a condition." Shifting her gaze to meet Edmund's, she stared at his bruised face and sighed. "Mayhap a meeting can be arranged in a few days. Would that suit you?"

He clenched his teeth as the needle pierced the open wound on his arm. Holding back the groan of pain, he said, "Aye. What of the bride you have selected for me?"

"We shall discuss that after you have your requested meeting with Mrs. Fernside."

"Thank you."

"Where was I before I let you distract me? Ah yes," she purred. "You mentioned Quinton is afraid of heights."

Grateful for something to concentrate on besides the methodical piercing of his skin and tug of the threads, he replied, "His face paled considerably before turning a bit green. I congratulated him as I descended the rope. He seemed shocked, but then acknowledged that he was afraid of heights when I pressed him."

"Thank you for confiding in me, Mr. Broadbank. I shall make a note of it and see that he is given another opportunity to succeed this evening."

Satisfied the man would receive a second chance, he nodded.

"Now then," Mrs. Dove-Lyon continued, "I believe two or three days will have the worst of the swelling on your face going down. I shall expect you on Wednesday, at two o'clock."

Edmund rose to his feet and held out his hand to her, for a moment forgetting the state of his palms.

Fortunately, Mrs. Dove-Lyon noted the bandages. "Snug, see that you take extra care cleansing those wounds. It would not do at all to have them go septic."

"Aye, Mrs. Dove-Lyon."

Her gaze met Edmund's. "Wednesday."

"Two o'clock," he replied. "Thank you."

She inclined her head and swept from the room.

"Formidable woman," Edmund remarked.

"That she is." Snug took hold of one of Edmund's wrists and guided him back over to the chair. "This is going to burn like the devil. Care for a swig?"

Edmund looked at the flask in the other man's hand and chuckled. "I may need more than one swig."

"WHAT IN THE bloody hell happened to you?" Colin demanded.

Edmund lifted the cool cloth from his face and snorted. "Ran into a fist repeatedly."

The viscount walked over to the sideboard, poured a healthy snifter of brandy, and carried it over to where his brother sat in front of the fire. Handing it to him, he asked, "Have you eaten?"

"Not hungry."

Before Edmund could sip from the glass, his brother snatched it away. "Food first, brandy second."

"Give me the damn snifter!"

Colin ignored him, strode over to the corner of the room, and yanked the bellpull. A few moments later, a discreet knock had the viscount opening the door. "Ah, Hanson. Please have Cook prepare a cold collation for my brother."

Leaning close to the viscount, Hanson said, "Your brother refused my offer of sending for your physician and Mrs. Pritchard's offer to have Cook prepare him a meal."

Colin glanced over his shoulder. "Edmund, you should have summoned me at once. Where did this footpad attack you on your way home this evening?" When his brother stared at him, Colin shook his head and told the butler, "Best send for the physician."

He shut the door behind Hanson and stalked over to where Edmund sat. "I have been waiting for the last few hours to hear what occurred while you were at the Lyon's Den. I had no idea you'd returned. Were you successful? Did you meet with our brother's mistress?"

"I'm to meet with her on Wednesday."

Colin studied him for long moments before asking, "Did someone try to shanghai you?"

"What makes you ask?"

"Bandages on your palms, weeping from where the skin blistered before it was torn away. Young sailors suffer from similar wounds while learning to climb the rigging."

"Did you?"

"Aye," Colin replied. "Burned like my hands were being held over a flame."

Edmund was surprised Colin admitted to experiencing pain. Things had changed since his brother married. "Won the first wager," Edmund said, "climbing to the top of the rope hanging from the ceiling in the main gambling room."

His brother lifted one eyebrow and whistled through his teeth. "A good twenty-foot climb. What happened to your face?"

"The third wager."

"Tell me about the second wager first."

"Fenced against Berges. He cheated."

"Do not know the man. Is he French?"

"No idea. But he did not follow the rules our gracious hostess outlined for our fencing bout. Three touches to the torso—no blood was to be drawn."

Colin reached for his brother's arm and let go immediately when he heard the hiss of pain. "Did it require stitches?"

"Aye. Snug took care of me."

"Why did she not send for a physician?"

"I told her not to."

"I take it the last bout involved your fists?"

"Aye. Bastard saw the bloody bandage around my upper arm and battered it a few times, hoping I'd quit."

Colin grinned. "From your swollen eye and purplish bruise on your jaw, I'd say you did not accommodate him."

"Right again!" Edmund grumbled. "Hand me that brandy, will you? I promise to eat when it arrives. Need something to dull the pain."

Colin obliged him, carefully handing over the snifter before sitting. "You'll need to soak your hands in a warm, salted water. They will heal faster."

"Snug mentioned it, but I was anxious to leave as soon as I was proclaimed the victor."

"Congratulations, brother. What of your bride?"

"I insisted on meeting with the actress first. Mrs. Dove-Lyon felt it best if I waited a few days, suggesting Wednesday. I accepted. As for my betrothed-to-be, apparently I shall be introduced to her after my meeting."

"The swelling should go down by then, but your hands..." Colin shook his head. "We'll see what the physician says. Barring any infection, you should be on the mend by then." He rose to his feet. "What is keeping—" A knock interrupted him. "Enter!"

"You really should think about lowering your voice, brother. It's reverberating in my skull."

Colin snorted out a laugh before striding to the door and opening it. "Thank you, Mrs. Pritchard." Before she entered the room, he motioned for the footman to place the tray on his desk and blocked her from entering. "Please send the physician in as soon as he arrives."

She watched the footman serving Edmund and then turned back to the viscount. She started to frown before inclining her head. "Of course, your lordship." Motioning for the footman to follow her, his housekeeper did as he bade.

"Bless Cook's heart," Edmund said, digging into the flaky crust of his favorite meat pie and groaning. "If I ignore the ache in my jaw, this savory pie will soon set my stomach to rights."

Reaching for the decanter of whiskey, the viscount poured two fingers and joined his brother in front of the fire. "Have you thought about where you will take up residence once you meet and marry your bride-to-be?"

Edmund paused in chewing. "Definitely not Moreland Chase."

Colin nearly snorted out his mouthful of whiskey before he agreed. "You and your bride are more than welcome to live here with us. Gemma offered, as a matter of fact."

"What of our niece or nephew? Will she welcome him? I need to know before I press the actress to allow him to spend time with us."

Colin smiled. "As a matter of fact, she's looking forward to it."

"She could probably use the practice."

Colin's face had a blank expression on it. "Practice?"

Edmund met his brother's gaze. "Has Gemma fully recovered from her bout of nausea?"

His brother frowned. "No, apparently she has been suffering in silence, but refuses to see the physician."

Edmund nodded. "Have you not noticed if she tires lately?"

"I have, and have ordered her to rest more."

Edmund nearly choked on a mouthful of pie. After clearing his throat, he mused, "I'm not certain ordering a woman about is ever a good idea."

"I do believe I shall speak to the physician about her recent nausea and exhaustion when he arrives."

"His answer might surprise you," Edmund remarked.

"Why?"

"Good God, Colin, if you cannot make an educated guess as to why your lovely wife has been nauseated upon rising and tires easily, I won't be telling you."

His brother's mouth hung open for a moment before he snapped it shut. "You don't suppose..." His eyes rounded in amazement. "Do you think...could she possibly..."

"I do suppose, and yes, I think she most definitely could be."

"A babe," Colin whispered. "We'd hoped..."

"Speak to the physician. Then I'd have a chat over breakfast and ask her outright."

"Should I wake her and have him examine her tonight?"

"It's late. Let her sleep."

"A babe," Colin whispered again.

The loud knock on the library door had the viscount jolting to his feet and striding to the door. "Come in, Dr. McIntyre!"

"What seems to be the—" The physician's gaze met Edmund's. "Any other injuries besides his face and head?"

"Aye," the viscount rumbled, "a slash on his upper arm, and his hands formed blisters before the skin tore."

"Odd…that sounds either like the burn from a flame…or mayhap from a rope."

Edmund glanced at his brother, satisfied by the closed expression on his face that he would not divulge where his brother had received the injuries.

When the viscount did not respond, the physician inclined his head. It was understood that unless the injury was dire and required explanation, the physician would not seek one. "Let's have a closer look."

Chapter Seven

"Mrs. Fernside," Titan announced, stepping back so that Adelaide could precede him into Mrs. Dove-Lyon's office.

"I have wonderful news for you." With the elegant sweep of her hand, the proprietress invited her guest to sit. "Your betrothed should be arriving shortly. I wanted to speak with you before he arrived."

Adelaide braced herself for whatever she was about to hear. Good or bad, she vowed to accept the news and move forward. She had given her word and the last of the coin she had scrimped and saved since coming to the decision to seek the aid of the Black Widow of Whitehall.

Hands folded demurely in her lap, her attention riveted on the veiled woman sitting behind the desk, she waited.

"There were quite a few offers for your hand, though only three men rose to the top of my list to be considered."

"I see." She had no idea what else to say. Should she ask what qualities the three men possessed that the others did not?

"Without going into detail as to how the final selection was made, or how candidates move up or down my list, suffice it to say, your betrothed was injured."

The bread and jam Miss Wythe had insisted Adelaide eat before leaving earlier that afternoon sat like a lump of lead in her belly. She fought back the emotions rioting inside of her to ask, "Is he under a physician's care?" Before Mrs. Dove-Lyon could respond, she quickly added, "I would like to be prepared to follow any instructions in the care of his injuries."

"His appearance is a bit startling, but I have his physician's assurance that other than keeping an eye out for infection and the removal of threads in a sennight, there are no further instructions."

Adelaide felt her head go a bit light. *Infection? Threads?* Just what had happened here at Lyon's Gate Manor?

"Drink this."

A short, squat glass was shoved into her hand. Obediently, she drank. The heat of the whiskey eased the tension in her throat enough for her to speak. "Thank you. Forgive me—I am more ill at ease than I thought."

"Do you plan to honor your word?"

Adelaide was surprised by the question. "I gave you my word, and I intend to keep it."

"No matter how shocking the injuries may be?"

She gathered her courage to ask, "Has he lost any limbs?"

"He has not."

"Well then, can you tell me what required threads?"

"I believe I shall let you and your betrothed meet. You may discuss them, if he so chooses. Not all gentlemen are willing to admit they have been injured, unless they're blatantly obvious...as a few of his injuries are."

A knock on the door had Adelaide setting down the glass, mindful not to spill the contents. The sip she had was enough.

"Come in."

The same gentleman who'd escorted her in appeared in the doorway. She found she was anxious to discover the name of her betrothed.

"Edmund Broadbank to see you."

Adelaide's heart thundered in her breast. *Broadbank?* Why would one of the earl's sons intrude now...right before she had the opportunity to meet with her intended? There must be some mistake. Would Mrs. Dove-Lyon go back on her word, or had the man arrived unexpectedly and barged in?

"Mrs. Dove-Lyon, always a pleasure."

The depth of his voice was surprisingly soothing.

"Mr. Broadbank, I'd like you to meet Mrs. Fernside."

She had no choice but to bow to convention and greet the man. Adelaide glanced up, and shock shot through her. His height and broad frame, combined with his rugged features and sculpted lips, captivated her.

He bowed but did not offer his hand to her. When he rose, she noticed the palms of his hands were wrapped with bandages. On second glance, she noted the bruising around one eye and along the line of his strong jaw. Her stomach churned. Mrs. Dove-Lyon had promised to find her a husband. She would not have conspired with this man to marry her off to one of little Adam's uncles...would she?

The man had either been in an accident, or her benefactress had lied to her. This man had obviously been injured...recently.

Fear threatened to overcome her. There could be no other explanation as to why he was here—now, when she was so close to changing the course of her life, about to meet the man whom she would wed...the man who would be a father to her sister's little one.

"A pleasure to meet you, Mrs. Fernside." His deep voice surrounded her. The roar in her ears increased as her gaze locked with his and she stared into eyes that mirrored the gray of a midwinter sky. Before she left, Lily had been delighted that her nephew shared the same eye color as his father...wintry gray eyes. Was it a family trait shared by the Broadbank brothers?

She managed to gather her composure and equilibrium enough to respond, "Mr. Broadbank."

"Forgive my appearance, Mrs. Fernside. I am not at my best."

"I am sorry for your…er…misfortune…or whatever occurred. I do hope you are not suffering any lasting effects."

His eyes brightened, changing their hue to a warmer shade of gray. "Thank you for your concern."

Needing to settle the problem of her marriage before speaking with the man, she inquired, "Would you mind terribly if we spoke another time? You see, I am to meet my intended and am a bit anxious to do so."

"As am I, after you answer a few pertinent questions—"

Mrs. Dove-Lyon interrupted, "Mr. Broadbank is your intended."

The two turned to stare at her with identical expressions of shock and dismay.

Broadbank's deep voice sounded threatening as he growled, "I beg your pardon? I thought I was to meet with the actress who was…involved…with my brother."

Actress? Involved? Adelaide opened her mouth to speak, but no words emerged. Was this some cruel joke? The man looming over her believed she was her sister and that she'd had an affair with his brother. What would Mrs. Dove-Lyon have to gain by mishandling their requests?

"I see this has come as a shock to you." He turned to glare at Mrs. Dove-Lyon. "I can say the same."

"As you both have agreed to the terms, I shall leave you two to get acquainted," the proprietress said. She swept from the room before either of them could argue.

"Do you mind if ask a few questions?" he asked Addy.

She shot to her feet as fear coursed through her.

"Are the rumors true? Is my brother Adam the father of your child?"

She sputtered, gasped, opened her mouth to speak, but no words emerged. The room began to spin at an alarming rate, forcing the edges of her vision to darken as she was pulled into a bottomless abyss.

EDMUND WATCHED THE young woman's eyes roll back in her head and swept her into his arms. Her slender form felt so fragile. Had she been starving? Was that what finally had her leaving her safe haven to seek Mrs. Dove-Lyon's assistance finding a suitable husband?

"Suitable. Bloody hell!"

Neither Berges nor Colgate would have been a suitable match for the lovely woman in his arms. Though slender, she was well formed, curvy where it counted. Loath to release her, he stared at the curve of her cheek, the arch of her brow. A honey-blonde lock of hair had slipped from its pins and stuck to the curve of her lashes.

Freeing it, he wondered if it was his question or the fact she had not expected to face the prospect of marrying her lover's brother that had sent her into a swoon.

She fit well in his arms. Snug against the breadth of his chest, her warmth seeped in all the way to his heart. No matter how she answered his question—whether or not she was his brother's former mistress—he would honor his word and take her to wife.

He brushed the tips of his fingers across her cheek. "Mrs. Fernside?"

Her eyelashes fluttered.

What words would urge her to open her eyes? Mayhap the same reason she'd ventured to the Lyon's Den...she sought security for herself and her babe.

"You are safe."

Her breathy moan sent his mind veering off in the wrong direction. He gathered his thoughts, preparing to state his case and the reasons why she should honor her word and the contract she'd signed.

"Won't you open your eyes for me?"

Her lashes fluttered again, and this time opened to reveal her lovely mermaid's eyes and the depth of her worry.

"I promise you are safe with me."

She nodded, but he doubted she believed him. "Please set me down?"

He carefully lowered her to her feet, but she swayed and reached out to steady herself. He slipped his arm around her tiny waist and helped her to sit. "Are you well? You've gone pale as flour."

"Just a bit overwhelmed."

Striving for a bit of levity, hoping it would ease some of her fear, he chuckled. "I have been known to have that effect in the past, though at the moment my handsome visage is a bit marred."

She stared at him for long moments before saying, "From the descriptions of your brother, you resemble him greatly."

"Descriptions?" When she merely lifted a shoulder in reply, he wondered if she was laying the groundwork for a fabrication. "One would think you'd never laid eyes on my brother."

The depth of her sorrow in her eyes troubled him.

"As the eldest brother, Adam was larger than life. He had a zest for living that could not be matched."

As if moved by his words, the widow—though he wondered if that too was part of her guise—placed her hand on his forearm, as if to comfort him. "Lily was truly in love with him."

"Who is Lily?"

She removed her hand at his sharp tone. "My sister."

Easing to his feet, he moved to stand behind the settee across from her. "If you are thinking to weave a web of lies, I warn you that Colin's connections have already rooted out the truth of who you are."

The sorrow disappeared and an emotion resembling fear replaced it, though he sensed the widow tried to hide the fact that she feared having the truth uncovered before they wed.

Hah! He would sooner marry a toothless hag!

"I fear Colin and his connections are off the mark. I am not the sister given to prevarications." Rising to her feet, she frowned at him. "Neither am I the sister who had an affair with your brother."

Shock had him wondering if it were possible. The description of her face and form...those entrancing sea siren's eyes... Reeling from the thought, he immediately dismissed it as another falsehood.

The click of the door as she fled had anger surging through him. He would not allow the woman to escape, nor would he allow her to discredit Coventry and King and slip through their fingers after a year spent trying to locate her!

By God, he would have the truth from her if it was the last thing he did!

Chapter Eight

His stride was much longer than his quarry's. He caught up to her by the door leading to the gardens. Thankful the establishment was empty due to the early hour, he called out to her, "Going somewhere?"

She spun around and glared at him. "I am leaving!"

He'd thought she would be frightened of him, but her expression had him wondering if she secreted a weapon on her person...though where, he could not begin to imagine.

"Mrs. Dove-Lyon's contracts have no loopholes," he warned. "If you signed one, you have no choice but to honor it."

Hands to her hips, she lifted her chin in challenge. The look of pure defiance only added to her beauty. He could understand how his brother had fallen hard for the entrancing woman's sister if she was anything like this one. Bloody hell, the woman had no idea of her appeal as she stood before him, trying to mirror his look of intimidation. She matched him frown for frown, and he had to call on his steely control not to be taken in by the lure in her siren's eyes.

He held out his arm to her. "Walk with me."

ADDY WANTED TO balk at the command, but the man was correct…she *had* agreed to Mrs. Dove-Lyon's terms, handed over the last of her coin, and signed her name to the document outlining those terms. Woe to her for not taking the time to read the blasted paper!

"Please?"

The tone of his voice had her looking up. What was it about the man that drew her in, compelling her to throw caution to the wind and follow him?

He stared at her. Eyes the dark gray of winter storm clouds changed to a lighter gray. She was reminded of April clouds that brought the life-giving, steady, soaking rain she and her tenant farmers needed to bless their crops.

She slipped her arm through his, surprised when he headed for the steps down into the gardens. Instead of being unsettling, the quiet eased the sharpest edges of her worries. When the silence between them continued, she sensed he was waiting for her to speak—to answer his questions.

"My sister Lily is an actress. She met your brother over a year ago while appearing on the stage at Covent Garden."

Though she could feel the tension radiating from him, he did not contradict her words. He led her over to a bench and eased her onto it.

"It was not what I had hoped or planned for my younger sister's future…to *tread the boards*—but she was so happy that I did not dare deny her."

"Why not?"

His confusion and the need to correct the misconceptions had Addy sharing the story of their parents' tragic accident. She related the details of their lives before losing their parents and being forced from their home by their cousin, the conditions of their grandmother's neglected estate she'd inherited, up to their last argument.

Expecting him to criticize her again for creating—how did he put it? Ah yes...a *web of lies*—she rose to her feet. "I know you do not believe me, but I—"

He raked a hand through his wavy, dark hair, and she could not help but smile at the way it stood on end before slowly falling back against his scalp. "No one could speak of the daily details of life on a small estate, dealing with tenant farmers, worrying over the weather and health of their crop, without having experienced it firsthand."

Her mouth gaped open for a moment before she realized it had and snapped it shut. "Have you?"

"Aye. My brother Adam and I often worked together at Moreland Chase. Though he would rather have been in London attending the many entertainments offered, including the theatre...especially Covent Garden. We thatched cottages, helped with repairs to his tenant farmers' barns and fencing, dug drainage ditches—most everything you have described and obviously experienced on your parents' and your grandmother's estates."

Hope sprang to life in her breast. He believed her! "It is not the life for everyone," she rasped. "Lily could not bear what she loftily referred to as the tedium of it. She has this need to be the center of attention. I blame myself for feeding it after we lost our parents and had to move out of the only home we'd known. Mayhap she would not have thrown herself into the gay and glittering life of an actress if I had insisted she do her part." Tears gathered, but she refused to let them fall. "I still cannot believe she would leave her babe behind—and cannot imagine what to tell him when he is older."

Sorrow was a double-edged sword at times. Would she ever let go of the blame she felt for her sister's choices—fame and the adoration of fans, engaging in an illicit affair, bearing a son out of wedlock?

Warm, strong hands gripped her upper arms. Shocked at the heat of his touch and the sparks that shot through her, she could not bring herself to meet his gaze.

"She had a son?"

The desperate rasp of his voice had her lifting her eyes to search his face. "Adam Strickland Broadbank III, after his father."

He pulled her into his arms and held her close. "We'd given up hope of ever solving the mystery." As quickly as he embraced her, he set her back from him. "Your sister is named Lily?"

"Lily Lovecote Fernside, though her stage name is Lily Lovecote. Her middle name is a family name."

"And your name is?

"Adelaide Dean Fernside."

"Dean is also a family name?"

"It is."

He swept the tips of his fingers along the curve of her cheek, and her heart trembled.

"My friends call me Addy."

He reached for her hands. "Beautiful Addy. I am sorry for not trusting you, but if you knew what we'd gone through trying to find you... From Father's description, and that of our staff who were present when you were turned away from Templeton House, it was assumed you were the actress."

"Lily was in no condition to travel. She suffered extreme nausea carrying your brother's child. When she finally confided his name, I felt it would ease her suffering and mayhap convince him to forgive her if he knew of their child. I was the one who made the journey to London hoping to speak to him."

"Forgive her?"

"She ended their affair when word reached her that he had been seen squiring an auburn-haired actress about town."

Edmund shook his head. "My brother was not known for lengthy relationships." The intensity in his eyes beseeched her to listen as he continued, "If he had known there was a child, he would have gone to Lily on bended knee to ask for forgiveness. He would have married her and wanted their son to be raised as the heir to the viscountcy."

"Mrs. Dove-Lyon mentioned meeting you and your brother, Colin. It sounds as if putting the title and well-being of family is a family trait that runs deep."

He squared his shoulders. "My brothers and I would do anything for our family. Now, we'd best go find Mrs. Dove-Lyon. She will not be pleased if she returns to her private office to find it empty."

"What will you tell the viscount's connections? I do not wish you to share all I have confided in you."

"The truth of our nephew's parentage is important. Without confirmation of it, we will not be able to protect him from being returned to his mother if she changes her mind."

"I was thinking only of her reputation if word gets out that she is a mother. You must understand that Lily does not have the time or inclination to care for her son. Why would she change her mind?"

"If her new protector thought it would be to his advantage to be stepfather to the heir to the Moreland viscountcy, he may be able to sway your sister."

An oily feeling churned in her belly and threatened to rush up her throat. Would Lily change her mind? "My sister is far too busy with rehearsals, performing, and the late-night engagements after performances to have the time to take proper care of Adam."

"I never said your sister would be the one caring for our nephew."

Her knees wobbled as his words sent a thrill through her. It was the second time he said, it, *Our nephew...*

Steadying her, he rasped, "Forgive me. My forthright way of speaking must have shocked you. It is something you must grow accustomed to. We Broadbank men are known for our plain speaking."

"After Lily's subterfuge, it is a welcome change."

"Did your sister leave a note asking you to take care of her babe—temporarily or permanently?"

Her breath hitched as she recalled the shock it had caused. "She did."

"Do you still have it?"

"Aye, but why do you ask?"

"It will ensure that no one will try to take Adam from us."

Hope once again filled her, easing the strain of the last few months. "Us?"

"Aye, you agreed to marry Mrs. Dove-Lyon's choice of husbands, did you not?"

She sighed. "You know I did."

"Apparently I am that choice—as you are hers for me. Marry me, Addy—ensure that our nephew will be raised to inherit the title my brother Adam would have insisted he have, had my brother lived."

"Will you promise to treat him as if he were your own?"

"Adelaide Dean Fernside, you have my oath of honor that I will raise him as my own son and teach him everything he needs to know to follow in his father's footsteps."

Worry filled her heart. "Will you love him?"

He surprised her by pressing his lips to her forehead. "I already do."

He slipped his arm around her waist, as her heart silently asked, *Will you love me too?*

Chapter Nine

A SATISFIED MRS. Dove-Lyon sent them on their way. Final terms had been agreed to and coin exchanged, with their assurance they would marry the following evening.

As he handed Addy into his carriage, Edmund's mind raced with all he had learned. The woman who'd begged an audience with his eldest brother last year was not the actress…but her sister. After speaking to her and learning more about her background, and her sister's, he was confident that she was telling the truth. Not even a hint of avarice had been evident in the depths of Addy's changeable blue-green eyes. He believed her.

As they bowled along London's streets, he devised a plan of action: Collect his nephew and retrieve Lily's letter giving her babe into her sister's care. Introduce Addy to Colin, Gemma, and their staff. Arrange a meeting with his brother, Coventry, and King to sort out the details and correct the misinformation. Marry by special license tomorrow evening.

Addy's touch startled him from his deep thoughts. Had she been speaking to him? "I beg your pardon. I was sorting through what needs to be done before we wed on the morrow."

"Our nephew's life has been through so many changes in the last year. Though he was only a few months old when he was left in my care, he may have been cognizant of his mother leaving on some level."

Edmund supposed she could be correct in that assumption.

Before he could question or make a comment, she continued, "Once I made the difficult decision that I would need to marry to protect and provide for Adam, our lives have been a bit chaotic. He is such a sweet little boy. I hope you will give him a chance to settle into our new life."

Did she just question the very fiber of my being? "I believe there is something of import we need to clarify before we reach your lodgings."

Her eyes mirrored the depths of her concern and worry. Edmund was man enough to admit his immediate reaction to her searching gaze was to assure her all would be well and that he was not an ogre. But deep down he knew they had to come to an accord as to the underlying essential issue of trust.

"I do not give my word lightly, and hold myself accountable to whatever I say I will do," he said. "That includes whether or not I will help repair the thatching for one of the tenant farmers at Moreland Chase, promising to find the woman who sought an audience with my eldest brother then promptly disappeared, or honoring my word to marry whomever Mrs. Dove-Lyon chose as my intended."

Addy bit her bottom lip and looked away. With his gloved finger, he gently touched the tip of her chin, redirecting her gaze to meet his once more.

"I have told you I believe you are who you have professed to be. I would think you would do the same for me and put your trust in me."

"It isn't that…exactly."

He nearly bit out the command to tell him what it was—*exactly*. Edmund drew in a calming breath, exhaled, and asked, "Have I given you reason not to trust my word?"

"I do not trust easily. This is all so unexpected, and everything is happening so quickly."

"Isn't that what Mrs. Dove-Lyon explained would happen, an immediate marriage, or marriage within a sennight?"

"Er...yes, actually, it was."

"Is there something that happened between my brother and your sister to engender your mistrust of anyone related to him?"

What in the bloody hell urged him to ask such a question? His brother had been forthright and honest in all of the dealings Edmund was a party to regarding Moreland Chase. Was there another side to his brother...that part of him that had been groomed to be the next Earl Templeton from birth?

Addy's barely audible sigh had Edmund reaching for her hand. He was unnerved by the lack of heat he'd expected to radiate through the thin layer of her kidskin gloves.

"If we are to get on, there can be no secrets between us. Trust is everything, Adelaide. Without it, our marriage does not have a bloody chance in hell of surviving."

She snatched her hand from his and crossed her arms beneath her bosom. He didn't know whether to be shocked or amused. Having been present on more than one occasion where Colin had said something that vexed his wife, he sensed that amusement would not be the proper response.

"Forgive me if my language has offended you."

She inclined her head.

"You have to see the rightness of my words—if not, then mayhap I shall have to bargain with Mrs. Dove-Lyon to dissolve our agreement and pay her double to do so."

Her every thought flitted across her face. When it appeared that she may lose her composure, he reached for her hand. He gave it a reassuring squeeze.

"I do see the rightness and agree that truth is essential," she said. "I still am not certain if all that Lily has told me *was* the truth."

He withdrew the linen square from his waistcoat pocket and pressed it into her hand, never letting go of the one he held. Edmund nearly released her hand to remove their gloves to take the chill from hers but decided that notion was too forward. His bride-to-be would no doubt be shocked.

"You're chilled, Addy."

She nodded.

Unsure of her willingness to allow more than what would be chivalrous, he removed his frockcoat and draped it around her slender shoulders, then rubbed her arms for a moment to warm her. "Now then. We have a bit of time before we arrive—why don't you tell me what concerns you?"

ADDY QUESTIONED HER decision to even speak of the fear she held close to her heart. What would Edmund do if she shared it with him? Would he order the driver to turn his carriage around and dump her back on Cleveland Row?

Glancing into his eyes, she saw something she had not expected…compassion.

"I have recently discovered that my sister has not been truthful about our upbringing or parentage."

His gut churning, and his apprehension growing, he nodded for her to continue.

"As an actress, she felt the need to rewrite her life story." Addy shifted to face him, and his coat slipped from her shoulders.

He reached out and settled it about her once more.

"Thank you. I was chilled."

"I thought as much. Please," he urged, "continue."

"Apparently, she is an orphan." Emotions swirled inside of her. She did not know which emotion to give in to—anger or tears. She could not give into either in front of the man she had come to see as her savior. The man who promised to raise her nephew and treat him as if he were his own.

Sinking into the warmth of his frockcoat, she murmured, "Lily claimed to have been raised by an elderly gardener and his wife in the country. When they passed away, she was left on her own again and decided to try her hand at becoming an actress at one of the Royal Theatres in London."

Edmund's brows rose, but he did not comment. Was he afraid she would tell him something even more troubling?

When she fell silent, unable to say more, he asked, "Is that all?"

Her belly clenched in fear, but she ignored it. She owed this man the truth. If he was outraged, it was not something she could control. Her actions and the way she would share what she learned were within her power to control. "While she was in labor, Lily blurted out another man's name."

Edmund tensed but did not interrupt her.

She worried that his reaction was merely delayed, and rushed to finish. "My sister was juggling affairs with another man and your brother. If I had known, I never would have traveled to London to speak with your brother." Twisting the handkerchief into knots, she whispered, "I have never been so ashamed as I was in that moment."

His stony gaze worried her. She confessed, "I would not blame you if you turned the carriage around and dropped me off on the sidewalk in front of Lyon's Gate Manor. I'm sorry I did not tell you before we left, but I was hoping you would meet Adam and see something familiar in his dear little features. Mayhap the color of his eyes would prove Lily's claim that your brother was the father."

When he turned to stare out of the window, she did the same. There was nothing more she could do. She had held back vital information from him and bared her sister's immoral conduct to him. There was a very good chance her nephew was not related to the Broadbank family at all, but the moment she'd laid eyes on Edmund and saw the family resemblance... Unless Edmund did not resemble his brother?

She dug deep for courage. "I am sorry for withholding part of the truth from you, Edmund." When he did not respond or turn to face her, she added, "I know it is too much to ask, but would you kindly let me off at the next street corner? It is not too far to walk from there to where my nephew and I are staying."

He gave instructions to his coachman, who slowed to a stop as she requested.

Without waiting for assistance, she opened the door and stepped down from the carriage. No need to add to her heartache at what could have been by glancing over her shoulder to see if he deigned to watch her walk away.

Quickening her pace to distance herself from the biggest mistake of her life, she chastised herself and her actions. She did not deserve his kindness. She dashed along the sidewalk as if she could outrun the devastating facts she'd withheld from Edmund, and realized her actions were on par with her sister's.

A lie of omission is still a lie.

Her steps determined, her resolve firm, she slowed to a normal pace. Chilled to the bone, she reached for the coat as it slipped off one shoulder, and gasped.

She had forgotten to return his coat!

Chapter Ten

Edmund was still absorbing her words when she exited the carriage. As the coachman snapped the reins, he told the man to wait. The carriage was still rocking to a stop, but that did not deter him from leaping to the curb to follow her.

How could she share such startling facts with him and then not stay long enough for him to digest her words? *Bloody hell!* This was a damnable situation! Addy obviously feared his wrath but had hoped he would see this through to the end and meet her nephew. And although he was not quite as certain as he had been, there was still the distinct possibility he was *their* nephew.

His stride long, his steps sure, he rapidly covered the ground between them. She never once turned around to note he followed her. At one point she stopped in her tracks, shifted his coat more closely around her, then slowly continued. She hunched over and wasn't paying attention to where she walked. Needing time to decide what to say to her, he matched her pace as he mulled it over.

God's truth, he had no idea what he intended to say to her. He knew one thing—he owed it to his brothers and, bloody hell, their father to see this through and meet the actress' son…the little one she'd named after the man she proclaimed was the father.

There was no help for the mass of uncertainty curdling in his gut. With a will of iron, he ignored it and quickened his steps, closing the distance between them.

"I believe you have my frockcoat."

Addy whirled around. Guilt and anguish evident in the depths of her eyes. Edmund sensed what she had done was not to save her sister's pride—it had been to protect the nephew she had been forced to raise on her own.

He held out his hand to her. "May I?"

Her confusion was endearing. He nodded toward the linen clutched in her hand. She drew in a breath and handed it to him. Gently, as if she would break, he blotted her tears and handed the handkerchief back to her.

Addy's uncertainty was evident in the way she watched him and took one step back, and then another, prepared to flee.

Edmund did not have the time to engage in a battle of wits or discussions of right and wrong. He had to find out if the little boy was related to him.

He offered his arm to her. After squinting up at him, she finally acquiesced and slipped her arm through his.

"Which building are you staying in?" he asked.

When she did not respond right away, he searched for something to say that would appeal to her need to respond. Silently gauging the time, he realized it was nearly teatime.

"Is it much farther? I'm a bit parched and could use a cup of tea."

Her steps faltered as she turned toward him.

Moved by the emotions swirling in her changeable eyes, he said, "I could summon my coachman. We could ride the rest of the way if it is much farther than the end of the block."

Addy finally said, "Another few blocks and we will be there."

"I shall have to add 'stubborn' to the list of attributes Mrs. Dove-

Lyon indicated my intended would have."

When her mouth rounded in a perfect O, Edmund was tempted to press his lips to hers to see if they were tart or sweet. Firm or soft. He had much to ponder.

Lifting his hand into the air, he signaled for his coachman. When the carriage pulled up alongside of him, he opened the door and helped Addy inside. "You were chilled before you took it upon yourself to alight without assistance, or even bid me goodbye. We cannot have you falling ill." Once they were seated, he gave the signal to his coachman to drive. "While I do not condone your keeping the whole truth from me, I begin to see what might have motivated you to do so."

Addy was quick to respond, "I thought only of little Adam. Before I sought Mrs. Dove-Lyon's assistance, I had to be even more vigilant in my protection of him."

Immediately on guard, he asked, "May I ask what prompted this?"

"Mr. Wythe informed me that there have been a handful of strangers asking if he knew Lily Lovecote and where she lived."

Edmund wondered if those strangers had been working for Coventry or King. "I would be happy to speak to my brother's contacts to see if they sent men to inquire after her. Where is it again that you live?"

"Grandmother's estate, Thorne House, is near Leeds." She paused before continuing, "Should anything happen to me, it will of course go to Lily."

A warning slithered up Edmund's spine. "Is that all that has happened? A few strangers inquiring after your sister?"

"A few nights before we left on the mail coach, someone broke the latch on the kitchen window and shattered the glass."

Certainty filled Edmund—someone had intended to do Addy harm! There was motive, and there was opportunity.

"Did you hear the intruder? Was anyone harmed?"

Addy shook her head. "Mr. Wythe's foxhound must have caught

the stranger's scent. He started to howl. Jake is a wonderful hunting companion and has two very distinct howls—one when he is on the scent, another when he senses danger."

"Excellent traits in a hound."

"That's when I heard glass breaking. I opened the door, thinking to investigate, but Mrs. Wythe told me in no uncertain terms to go back inside and bolt the door, assuring me Mr. Wythe and his faithful hound would handle the matter."

He marveled at her courage. Something Mrs. Dove-Lyon had only briefly mentioned. "Did you do as she asked?"

Addy's glance slid to the side.

"What would you have been able to do that Mr. Wythe could not? Who would tend to your nephew if he woke up crying?"

"I was confident I could help-besides, Adam sleeps soundly." She frowned and appeared to be considering her next words with care. "Enough was enough. Between strangers asking questions and now someone trying to break into the house...I planned to surprise them." She lifted her chin, proclaiming, "I'm quite handy wielding a fireplace poker."

He nearly snorted with laughter, but at the dark look aimed at him, he swallowed the urge. "I hope you never have occasion to test that particular skill." When she fell silent, he prompted, "And?"

She sighed. "I did as she suggested."

"Ah, because you saw the sense in it."

Addy's eyes danced with merriment. "Nay. Adam chose that moment to wake up screaming."

It was Edmund's turn to find his mouth agape. Snapping it shut, he shook his head. "So much for his being a sound sleeper." Needing to make the woman see sense, he asked, "Whatever possessed you to hare after an intruder when our nephew so clearly needed protection? Must I remind you that you are the only relative that little one has who gives a bloody damn about him?"

She shook her head.

He made a split-second decision. The woman and her nephew needed looking after. It no longer mattered if the little one was his brother's son. Edmund planned to be the one to see to their protection and well-being.

He would bide his time and find the most opportune chance to mention his plans to Addy. She would have no choice but to agree. It was his brother and father who may need more time to become accustomed to his decision to marry, especially if it turned out his eldest brother was not the little boy's father.

Battling the unease that tangled with his worry that Addy, and therefore Adam, was the target of a nefarious plot, he said, "We will have much to discuss after you introduce me to your nephew."

Instead of balking at his comment, Addy inclined her head in silent agreement.

The carriage slowed and came to a halt a few moments later. He alighted first and handed her down. Time to meet the little one that would no doubt cause an uproar once his father learned of his existence. Edmund hoped Colin would see the rightness of what he planned to do before sending a missive to their father.

Addy led him into the alleyway between two shops and smiled. "We are staying with Mr. Wythe's older sister. Miss Wythe has rooms on the upper floor."

He opened the door and motioned for her to precede him.

"She always has the kettle on the boil."

"It will be a pleasure to meet Miss Wythe and be introduced to little Adam over a pot of tea."

Her smile reached her eyes and drew him into their depths until he was surrounded by her warmth and caring. He willingly accepted that he'd fallen under her spell and hoped to bloody hell he wasn't about to be dashed upon the rocks!

Chapter Eleven

If Miss Wythe was surprised to find Addy standing in the doorway wearing a gentleman's frockcoat, and a gentleman *sans* frockcoat standing beside her, she gave no indication of it.

She greeted Edmund without the least bit of hesitation once introduced. "Your family is quite well known in the Borderlands where I was raised, Mr. Broadbank. It is indeed a pleasure to receive you."

The little boy's eyes widened as he stared at Edmund. His lower lip trembled. Before he could cry, Addy scooped him up. Holding him close, she whispered nonsense words to soothe him as she castigated herself for not considering the effect Edmund's height and bruised face would have on one so small.

"There," she crooned, "you see, Mr. Broadbank is not so tall now that I've got you safe in my arms, is he, my love?"

Adam shook his head and slanted a look at the man who had fallen silent the moment their faces were close.

Edmund reached out as if to touch the little one's face, but changed his mind, dropping his hand to his side. Addy noted the way he stared at her nephew, taking in the distinct color of his eyes, the shape of his face. He had to agree the resemblance to himself was uncanny.

But she had never met Adam Broadbank. The question that had her heart pounding was one she was afraid to ask—did Edmund resemble his eldest brother, or did Adam look more like their mother, who had been rumored to be fair-haired, with green eyes? If that were the case, then her nephew could not be related to the Broadbanks at all.

When Edmund continued to stare at her nephew without speaking, she resolved to absolve him of any vows or promises made to their benefactress.

"I have had the kettle warming, and hoped you would return soon, Adelaide," Nora said. "Such a pleasure to meet your intended."

Addy spoke clearly, correcting the kindly woman's assumption. "I must have misunderstood Mrs. Dove-Lyon, Miss Wythe. I did not meet my intended today after all. Mr. Broadbank had a meeting with Mrs. Dove-Lyon and kindly offered to drop me home. It was…er…on his way."

The older woman's gaze shifted to Edmund and back. "Forgive me. I have the tendency to jump to conclusions. You are still more than welcome to stay for tea, Mr. Broadbank." With the humor Addy had come to appreciate, she added, "You must be chilled, having traveled without your frockcoat."

Edmund's eyes softened as he accepted the invitation. "That is most kind of you, Miss Wythe. It would be most appreciated, as I had not anticipated having to do the gentlemanly thing and offer my coat to Miss Fernside." Turning to Addy, he pointed to his coat. "May I?"

She tried not to stiffen as he removed his coat from her shoulders. After her declaration, she felt it best to remind him, "It is *Mrs.* Fernside."

"Ah, it is so easy to jump to conclusions and misunderstandings, isn't it?"

She was unsure of what exactly Edmund was referring to but decided it would be best to agree. "So it would seem."

"Please have a seat," Miss Wythe said. "I shall have this ready to pour in a moment."

He pulled out a chair for Addy, and she sat with Adam comfortably in her arms. She'd grown accustomed to having meals holding her nephew.

As she wondered when Edmund would be taking his leave, her heart wrenched at the knowledge that he would. She turned her attention to the little boy's chattering, wondering how in the world she could work up the wherewithal to have Mrs. Dove-Lyon select another husband for her—or what she would do if the woman demanded more coin.

EDMUND DID NOT bother to correct Addy's statement that he was not her intended, nor did he speak up when he'd recognized his eldest brother—and himself—in the engaging little boy chattering away in her arms. The bond between them was evident, as was their affection for one another. If he had passed the two when walking about the streets of London, he would assume they were mother and child from their actions alone. Though, in truth, the little boy bore no resemblance to her.

Miss Wythe placed the teapot and plate of scones on the table. "Now then, what did I forget... Ah, one moment while I pour a small cup of milk for Adam."

Edmund rose, waiting to seat her when she returned with the cup.

Her smile of delight pleased him, and he anticipated her reaction when he informed her that he *was* Adelaide's intended would be similar.

"Thank you, Mr. Broadbank."

"You are welcome." He returned to his seat.

As she poured and passed a sturdy cup and saucer to Addy, she inquired as to how he took his tea.

"A splash of cream, if you have it."

After doctoring his tea to his preference, she handed it to him. "I do hope you enjoy the cream scones—they are a family favorite."

"My brother's cook has a way with scones. I'd be delighted to sample yours."

He slid a glance at the woman seated beside him. She was smiling as she steadied Adam's cup while he sipped. She broke her scone into bite-sized pieces, and handed them to the boy one at a time while he continued with his happy chatter.

"Mrs. Fernside, I fear I must contradict your words."

Her startled eyes widened. "My words?"

"Mrs. Dove-Lyon more than met my requirements in a wife when she introduced us. Did you forget our plans to marry tomorrow evening?"

The shock of his pronouncement rendered her silent. He fought against the urge to chuckle, assuming it would not be well done of him.

Turning to their hostess, he shook his head. "It would appear that Mrs. Fernside has quite forgotten her promise to marry me on the morrow."

"No! That is to say, I had not forgotten," Addy said. "I assumed you had changed your mind."

"I have not changed my mind."

Doubt and worry swirled in the depths of her lovely eyes. He had been the one to place them there, and he would be the one to erase them.

"The resemblance is astounding. In our family, it is customary to have portraits painted of the heir apparent at various stages of his life. I have seen miniatures of my brother as an infant and right around this young man's age. Colin and Father will have no choice but to accept the fact he is our nephew and rightful heir to the viscountcy."

The clatter of her teacup crashing against her saucer broke the silence.

"Oh dear," Miss Wythe said, rising to her feet. "Let me clear that away while you change Adam."

From the tone of the older woman's voice, it was not a request. Addy rose to do her bidding. When the door to what must be the room she shared with the little one closed, Edmund said, "I will do all in my power to protect and care for Adelaide and Adam. You have my word of honor."

Miss Wythe deposited the broken bits of the teacup and saucer in the rubbish bin and wiped her hands on a drying cloth. "Have you given the same pledge to Adelaide?"

"I have."

"Yet for some reason, she did not believe you."

The woman was obviously trying to pry what was none of her concern from his lips. Because of the obvious friendship between the women, he decided to offer a partial explanation. "Adelaide and I were having a conversation in my carriage when she shared information that surprised me. Apparently, when I did not react immediately, she asked to stop the carriage and exited before I had time to gather my response to her."

Miss Wythe narrowed her eyes and studied him in silence. "What did she tell you?"

"That is between Mrs. Fernside and myself. If you wish to know, you will have to question her."

"I believe I shall. Kindly make yourself comfortable while I speak with her."

Mrs. Wythe bustled past him, knocked on the closed door, was admitted, and shut the door behind her.

He could hear muffled voices and the delighted sounds of his nephew—there was no longer a question in his mind that Adam was his family. With a heavy sigh, he admitted aloud, "That did not go exactly as I'd planned."

He would have to do a bit of back-pedaling if he were to get Addy to agree to accompany him to Templeton House today. The unsettling notion that she would refuse him today or tomorrow—or marry him at all—had him clenching his jaw.

I will not allow her to slip through my fingers a second time! He thought of the inroads they had made getting to know a bit about one another, first in the garden, and then on the ride to her lodgings—until her confession that she'd hidden essential information about her sister's affairs.

"She thought only of protecting Adam," he said aloud.

"I am glad you have come to the correct conclusion. Everything I have done was to protect my sister and her unborn babe."

He hid his surprise. He had not heard her footsteps. When he opened his mouth to speak, she placed a hand on his arm. He closed his mouth and waited for her to continue.

"My life changed forever when Adam was born. I devoted myself to helping my sister care for him, and then took over his care the day she left us. I will marry you, because I trust that you are capable of protecting him from whomever broke into Thorne House."

He frowned at the notion that that would be all she sought from their union. "And if I wish our marriage to be more than words on a scrap of parchment?"

Her inability to speak was answer enough for now. She had not even considered the possibility that he would be attracted to her and want their marriage to be more than a convenience for his family.

He reached for her hand and brought it to his lips. "I can see that I will have to woo you and convince you of the benefits of a true marriage with me." He let his lips linger a moment longer than was proper, savoring her satin-smooth skin and faint scent of lavender.

She finally found her voice. "Given my reasons for needing to marry, I thought our marriage would be in name only."

Her hesitation was not born of fear—it was uncertainty. He would need to plan his seduction of his bride-to-be carefully.

With a gentle tug, he brought her closer. Lifting her hand once again, he brushed a kiss across one knuckle at a time, watching her eyes widen and the pulse in the hollow of her throat quicken as her cheeks pinkened.

"I believe you and I will enjoy the time spent getting to know one another better." He turned her hand over and placed a succulent kiss to the palm of her hand, sampling the flavor of her skin with the tip of his tongue.

Her soft moan of surprise was echoed by the shocked pleasure in her siren's eyes.

Delighted with her reaction, and the passion he sensed lay dormant within the beautiful woman he would marry on the morrow, he said, "It shall be my duty and pleasure to ensure that we do. To prove I am a man of my word, I shall let you set the pace."

When her eyes glazed over and she swayed toward him, he locked his arm around her and pulled her into his embrace.

"Trust me, Addy."

Chapter Twelve

Edmund stepped down from the carriage and held out his arms. The imp in his fiancée's arms shook his head and clung to Addy, whose light laughter smoothed over the situation.

"Hang on tight now, Adam." She smiled at the man patiently waiting for her to alight, her stubborn nephew clinging to her like a burr. "Adam isn't used to strangers," she quickly explained as she joined Edmund on the sidewalk. "We did not have many visitors at Thorne House."

Adam hid his face in the crook of her neck, refusing to look at Edmund.

"I admit, I'm not accustomed to young children, but will acquiesce to whatever you suggest until he accepts me," Edmund said.

Warmth filled her. It was going to be all right.

Edmund placed his hand at the small of her back as the front door opened. "Welcome to Templeton House, Addy. Come and meet my family."

"Welcome home, sir!" the butler said.

"Thank you, Hanson."

The servant ushered them inside and reached for Addy's coat, only to stop at the little one's cry.

"The boy is a bit shy, Hanson." Turning to Addy, Edmund asked, "Do you think Adam would prefer to be set down?"

She beamed. "I believe he would." Used to the little one's shy moods, she coaxed him to let go of her neck and bent down to set him on his feet.

"What is the meaning of all that caterwauling, Hanson?" a man said, entering the hallway.

The butler was in the process of helping Addy remove her coat as he staunchly replied, "Mrs. Fernside's nephew is quite shy. Something must have startled him."

Addy bent down to pull Adam into her arms to soothe him, relieved that the butler tried to protect him too.

To her shock, Edmund snorted with laughter. "Leave off, Colin. You're scaring our nephew."

The man striding toward them was equal in stature and just as broad as the man she'd promised to wed. His dark hair and wintry-gray eyes marked him as Edmund's brother. The resemblance to her nephew was striking. Obviously Colin thought so, too.

His gaze settled on the boy in her arms, he proclaimed, "I thought you were bringing your intended home?"

Adam started to cry. As Addy brushed his tears away, she glared at Colin.

Before she could remonstrate him, Edmund said, "You are not at sea in a storm, brother. Lower the volume, if you would."

Colin cleared his throat. "Forgive me. It must be the shock of seeing our nephew for the first time. We didn't believe your claims—"

Addy's sharply indrawn breath had Edmund interrupting, "Hanson, please let Mrs. Pritchard know that Mrs. Fernside and her nephew have arrived and will be staying with us."

Hanson's face remained expressionless as he responded, "Very good, sir. Shall I inform Cook that there will be one more for dinner?"

Edmund nodded and turned to his brother. "Allow me to introduce my intended, Mrs. Adelaide Fernside, and her nephew, Adam. Addy, meet my brother Colin, Viscount Moreland."

Addy had not been certain what type of reception she would receive at Templeton House, but the viscount with the sea captain's voice bowing before her was a surprise.

"Intended, you say?" Colin said. "It's a pleasure, Mrs. Fernside." With a glance at his brother, the viscount continued, "You did not mention a widow—"

Edmund muttered something she could not quite hear as he placed his hand on the small of her back. "I believe Gemma would enjoy meeting my intended, don't you?"

His brother swore beneath his breath before he strode to the foot of the staircase and bellowed his wife's name.

Addy placed her hand to Adam's ear, but it was too late—the viscount's booming voice had startled him into wailing. "I beg your pardon, your lordship, but would you kindly cease from shouting inside? It is upsetting Adam."

The viscount's mouth gaped open as his eyes widened in disbelief. "Did you just command me to stop shouting?"

Addy frowned at him. "You know very well I did not command you to do anything. I begged your pardon before asking you to cease using such an inappropriate volume of speaking inside."

"Colin, whatever am I to do with you?" said a woman coming downstairs.

"*Gemma,*" Colin said.

Addy's ire evaporated. The frustration evident on the viscount's face as he glared at the lovely woman worried her. "I apologize for upsetting you, your lordship, but—"

"You are not the one who should apologize," Gemma said. "Colin, you really must pay heed to the fact that we are not onboard your ship, lest everyone in our household shall have to take to filling their ears with cotton batting."

Edmund's laughter rang out, and Addy could not help but smile at the masculine timbre of the sound. "Gemma, allow me to introduce my intended, Mrs. Adelaide Fernside, and her nephew, Adam. Addy, my sister-in-law Gemma, Viscountess Moreland."

"It is a pleasure to meet you, your ladyship," Addy said.

"Please, call me Gemma—after all, we are soon to be related." With a warm smile, the viscountess whispered, "I am sure Cook has something sweet to eat, Adam—shall we go find out?"

When Adam nodded, Gemma and Addy smiled.

"Follow me."

WATCHING THE WOMEN retreat, Edmund spun to face his brother. "Have you no sense of propriety asking such questions where all and sundry are present to hear?"

"You could have warned me," Colin grumbled. "Why are you marrying our brother's lover?"

Edmund clenched his hands into fists at his sides, quelling the need to strike his brother. Instead, he strode down the long hallway to the library. Not waiting for one of the footmen to open the door, he yanked it open and stalked inside.

When his brother closed the door behind him, Edmund rounded on him. "Firstly, she is not the actress, nor was she our brother's former lover."

"Do you have proof of that?"

"She has shared how she came to have the care of our nephew, and I believe her."

Colin frowned. "You have been taken in and bewitched by her

mermaid's eyes. Do you have proof of her claims?"

"She brought it with her."

Taken aback by the response, Colin asked, "What kind of proof does she have?"

"A letter from her sister, Lily Lovecote, an actress currently affiliated with the Theatre Royal, Covent Garden."

Colin clasped his hands behind his back and paced.

Used to his brother's need to pace as he had obviously done during his years in the Royal Navy, Edmund did not bother to ask him to stop.

"What did the letter say?"

"I believe—"

Colin jolted to a stop, growling, "You haven't seen the proof?"

Edmund met his brother's fierce glare with one of his own. "I bloody well did not have the time."

"How do you know she isn't lying? Good God, Edmund, from the strong Broadbank family resemblance, the boy could be your son...or mine!"

"I hadn't thought of that." When his brother opened his mouth to speak, Edmund rushed on, "I don't have the time to explain my reasons for believing Addy. There have been a few strangers who stopped at her grandmother's house asking questions about the actress—her sister Lily Lovecote."

"They could have been Coventry or King's men doing what we hired them to do."

"I am well aware, but a few nights later, someone tried to break into Thorne House well after midnight."

The viscount's face hardened. "Whoever it is must be brought to light! They must know that her son—"

"Nephew!"

Colin raked a hand through his hair, much the same as Edmund was wont to do when highly agitated. "Her nephew is heir to the viscountcy. We must protect him at all costs!"

"Adam would have expected no less," Edmund replied.

His brother placed a hand on Edmund's shoulder. "Are you willing to give up your chance at happiness to offer the protection of your name and consequence to our nephew and his aunt?"

"Without question—but you should know, Colin, I have strong feelings for Addy."

"Do you?"

"I plan to woo her and win her affections. I'll not stand for a marriage of convenience. We both know our parents shared a distant affection. I want more… I want what you and Gemma have."

The expression in Colin's eyes changed to one of deep affection. "I cannot imagine my life without the lass in it. We need to send a missive to Coventry, and one to King. It would be best to have their assurances that the intruder was not connected to their search for the missing actress."

"I will see if Addy is up to meeting with them."

"Is that wise?"

"My wife and I will have no secrets between us."

Colin chuckled. "She's not your wife yet."

Edmund grinned. "She will be by this time tomorrow."

Hanson was summoned, and missives were sent to Captain Coventry and Gavin King of the Bow Street Runners.

The brothers shared a glance as the sealed missives were entrusted to two retired seamen. "Are you certain Perkins and Grant won't be detained by King?" Edmund asked. "They have a dangerous air about them."

The viscount chuckled. "Exactly why I hired them a fortnight ago when I received word they retired from the navy. King met them last year. You must remember meeting them when that madman held *my* bride-to-be at gunpoint."

How could Edmund forget what had transpired, or how brave his sister-in-law had been?

Colin continued, "I trust them with Gemma's life—and that of your bride-to-be."

Gratitude filled Edmund. His brother may be gruff, and may not have retained all of the social graces their mother had tried to instill in them, but he was one of the few men Edmund trusted to guard his back—and his family-to-be. "Then I shall trust them with Addy and Adam's, although I wouldn't mind the opportunity to speak to them when they return."

Colin's booming laugh echoed through the room. "And so you shall, brother. So you shall."

Chapter Thirteen

"Thank you for your kindness, your ladyship." Gemma's airy laughter surrounded Addy as they chatted in the upstairs sitting room. "Please, call me Gemma."

"Er...thank you, Gemma. We are so fortunate the viscount did not demand we leave the premises as I had been..." Addy trailed off. She should not have said anything. What would the viscountess have to say when she learned of Lily's affair with the viscount's brother? Would she be the one to show Addy and her precious nephew to the door?

But Gemma gently patted her hand. "Whatever worry you carry appears to be a heavy burden. When you are ready, I'm more than happy to listen."

"Your lady—"

"Gemma," the viscountess reminded her.

"I do not know when or if I could. Not all families are as close and caring as yours."

Gemma frowned. "My father all but sold me to the highest bidder and tried to send my younger brother to America in order to add our inheritances to his wealth."

Addy was not shocked by the viscountess' disclosure. She had her own tale of family woe. "That must have been absolutely frightening! But the viscount seems to have a great affection for you."

Gemma smiled. "The affection is mutual. Colin rescued me…and my brother."

"I am happy to hear that. Edmund has vowed little Adam and I will have the protection of his name, but I'm not certain it is fair to him. What will he gain from the bargain?"

Gemma rose from her seat and walked over to her dressing table, returning with a small looking glass. "Take a look and see what my brother-in-law will be gaining."

Addy frowned at her reflection. "A tired spinster who has long been on the shelf and her motherless nephew."

Gemma glanced over her shoulder to where little Adam napped under a coverlet on the settee. "He is not motherless," she said. "He has you."

Emotion clogged her throat, sensing Gemma did not say such to make her feel better. "I tried my best to raise my sister," Addy said. "But failed by indulging her every whim."

"It is so hard when they turn that imploring gaze upon you and you simply cannot do otherwise but say yes."

Addy met Gemma's gaze. "How did you know?"

Gemma sighed. "I am guilty of doing the same. After our mother died, I coddled my younger brother, much to our father's dismay. He wanted to form him into a miniature version of himself."

"My sister craved attention then, as she still does, performing before adoring fans at Covent Garden. When she fell ill, I thought it was a wasting disease, she lost so much weight, but then she started to gain it back…and then some."

"We have done what we thought best at the time, Addy. If you distance yourself for a moment from the past and the choices you made, can you think of any other way you would have reacted? Would you have let your sister flounder to find her way without your help?"

"I would do anything for Lily."

"As I would do anything for Simon."

Adam made a snuffling sound in his sleep.

"He is the dearest little boy," Addy said. "I cannot imagine how my sister could turn him over to me."

"What would his life have been like if she dragged him along to rehearsals and performances?"

"For a short time, she did take him with her while she was rehearsing, but he cried when they would leave and would be crying when they returned. It broke my heart, so I pressed her to leave him with me while she was performing." Her sigh was filled with regret. "Mayhap if I hadn't—"

"Adam would have suffered not being doted on by his loving aunt."

"Thank you, Gemma. You have no idea what your kind words mean to me."

"Kindred spirits must support one another."

A knock on the door interrupted their quiet discussion.

"Come in," Gemma called.

"Dinner will be served in a quarter of an hour, your ladyship."

"Thank you, Hanson." When the butler left, she asked, "Are you certain you won't join us for dinner, Addy?"

"I think Adam needs more time to get to know your housekeeper before I leave him alone with her. We shall be fine dining in the lovely bedchamber you have readied for us." When Gemma hesitated, Addy assured her, "I promise we won't make a mess."

The viscountess smiled. "It is not that. I do wonder if Edmund would approve of his bride-to-be dining alone."

Just then, Adam opened his eyes and gave a cry of dismay. Addy rose and lifted him into her arms. "I'm not alone, Gemma. I have Adam."

"And after tomorrow, you will have Edmund, Colin, and I."

"I do not know how Mrs. Dove-Lyon managed to find both a husband and a family for me, but—" Addy paused at the curious expression on her new friend's face. "What's wrong? Are you ill?"

Gemma shook her head. "Did Edmund mention how Colin and I met?"

"No, but you did say your husband rescued you."

"Aye, he rescued me at the Lyon's Den."

Addy slowly smiled, feeling truly at ease for the first time since entering Templeton House. "It would appear we have more in common than we realized."

"Even more reason to share our worries and woes with one another," Gemma told her. "I was judged harshly after I met and married Colin. No matter what has happened in the past, or what may happen in the future, I promise never to do that to you."

Addy pressed a kiss to the sleepy little one's head. "You have my vow that I will do the same—and more, will stand by your side through thick and thin."

The two women were beaming when Mrs. Pritchard rushed into the room to remind the viscountess the men were patiently waiting for them.

Gemma laughed. "I highly doubt my darling husband has ever waited patiently for anyone."

Mrs. Pritchard's eyes twinkled with amusement, though she did not agree or disagree. "After you, your ladyship." When Addy made no move to follow, she inquired, "Are you not feeling well, Mrs. Fernside?"

"I'm fine," Addy was quick to respond. "Her ladyship has kindly agreed that Adam would be more comfortable eating with just us two until he becomes more accustomed to our new surroundings."

"Will you be eating here?"

Gemma said, "I sent the request down to Cook, asking for a tray to be delivered to Mrs. Fernside in her bedchamber."

"Very good. If you'll follow me, I shall escort you."

Addy declined. "That is most kind, but I remember which room you have graciously put us in. Please don't keep the men waiting on my account."

Gemma hugged Addy, brushed the tips of her fingers across Adam's sleep-tousled hair, and promised to see her after dinner.

Watching them leave, Addy pressed a kiss to Adam's forehead and asked, "Are you hungry?"

Adam smiled. "Cake?"

Addy laughed and made her way to their bedchamber. Bolstered by Gemma's offer of friendship and her marriage to Edmund the following day, she finally felt as if all was right with her world.

EDMUND STOOD IN the open doorway smiling to himself as he listened to the chatter he looked forward to becoming accustomed to. As Adam babbled, he realized it was going to be a bit more difficult to understand everything the little boy said. Addy had no problem deciphering the little man's garbled communication—a combination of made-up words and sounds—if her responses and smile were any indication.

Wondering if she'd be upset if she caught him eavesdropping, he cleared his throat to make his presence known.

She whirled around, hand to her throat. "Oh! Edmund, you startled me. I didn't know you were standing there. Have you been waiting long?"

He smiled at the worry in her lovely eyes and sought to ease it. "Long enough to wonder how long it will take me to even understand every other word. You seem to know exactly what Adam is saying."

Her lilting laughter floated around him like a cloud. "That is because we are facing one another. While I can understand most of the words he uses, what I cannot, I decipher from his facial expressions. He is such a happy little boy."

Edmund crossed the threshold, surprised when Adam raised his arms in the air and said, "Up!"

Unsure of himself, having never picked up a child before, Edmund whispered, "Maybe you should pick him up, and I'll watch closely to see how it's done."

Adam's expression changed from delight to sadness as tears filled his Broadbank-gray eyes.

"It's all right, dear one," Addy soothed, dropping to her knees in front of Adam. "Edmund has never picked up a little person before," she explained, speaking to him as if he were an adult. "It may be easier if you crouch down," she told Edmund.

When he did as she bade, she instructed him where to place his hands as he drew the little boy close to his chest.

Adam patted Edmund's cheek and babbled away. Settling the boy in the crook of his arm, Edmund slowly gained his feet as a strange feeling of contentment washed over him.

As if she understood, Abby rose and stood beside him. "It's a wonderful feeling, isn't it?"

Edmund thought he knew what she was referring to but needed to be certain. "What is?"

Addy placed the tip of her finger on the end of Adam's upturned nose. "How quickly the warmth of a child's love fills you."

His gaze met hers over the top of Adam's head. "Is that what I'm feeling? How can you be sure?"

Adam snuggled closer to him, and she smiled. "It's a magical bond that not everyone has the privilege of experiencing." Placing her hand on Adam's back, she sighed. "We have been blessed."

In that moment, holding Adam in his arms, with Addy standing so close to his side, Edmund knew he was meant to raise his nephew. He was meant to be this boy's father.

"I beg your pardon, sir?" Hanson asked, entering.

The spell was broken when Addy stepped back from him.

"Yes, Hanson?" Edmund said.

"His lordship has requested your presence, and that of Mrs. Fernside, in the library."

"As much as I would love to be accommodating, please tell my brother that I am unable to bow to his request."

A FEW MOMENTS later, the sound of heavy footfalls echoed through the entryway, accompanied by a loud grumbling.

"We'd best hurry before my brother forgets himself and bellows—"

"Where in the bloody hell are you, Edmund?"

Adam's face crumpled, as he wailed in response to Colin's booming question.

Handing him off to Addy, Edmund mumbled something about manners, pigs, and the Grace of God. Wise enough not to ask him to repeat himself, she soothed the little one in her arms and followed. She found Edmund leaning over the railing, giving his brother the verbal lashing he deserved.

The shock on the viscount's face had her stifling her laughter, but a giggle escaped. Eyes wide, lips pressed together to keep from emitting another sound, she waited for the viscount to turn his wrath on her.

Instead, he squared his shoulders, shook his head, and retreated toward the library.

"That was an unexpected reaction," Edmund said. "Well, we'd

best see what is so important." When Addy lifted her skirts with one hand, while carrying Adam on the opposite hip, he offered, "Why don't I carry him down? We wouldn't want either of you to fall."

She beamed, surprised by his kind offer, though after the way he'd held Adam to his heart and she witnessed the awe and pleasure on Edmund's face, she should not be. "Thank you."

He waited for her at the base of the stairs, offering his free arm. They heard the muffled voices as they approached the library. "Forgive me, Addy. I'd completely forgotten that my brother sent missives to Coventry and King."

"Acquaintances of yours?"

"Captain Gordon Coventry served in the Royal Navy and is a good friend to Colin. I've met him once or twice before Colin was forced to give up his captaincy to accept the title after our brother's death. Gavin King is with the Bow Street Runners and became acquainted with my brother when there was an incident involving Gemma before their wedding."

"Gemma told me that your brother rescued her at the Lyon's Den. I'd completely forgotten that Mrs. Dove-Lyon mentioned she made an excellent match for your brother."

"As ours will be," Edmund said. "I have watched the love grow stronger between Colin and Gemma. I hope this does not sound odd to you, but I believe marriage, like friendship, must be tended to enable it to blossom and grow." He paused outside the door to the library and faced her. "I would like ours to be a marriage we both will tend to, enabling love to grow as we raise Adam as if he were our own."

Hope twined with wonder at his words. He motioned for her to enter the room, then followed. Taking her hand, he said, "I'm sorry if you are not ready to hear—"

She rose on her toes and pressed a kiss to his cheek. "I would love that above all things, Edmund."

The door swung open, and the viscount grumbled, in a much softer voice than normal said, "You can kiss him later. Coventry and King have uncovered some startling information." Bowing to Addy, he murmured, "Forgive me for frightening Adam. I tend to forget I'm not on my quarterdeck."

She smiled at him. "There is nothing to forgive. We are new to your household. Adam and I are most grateful for the warm welcome, your lordship. I imagine it will be a bit of an adjustment for all of us."

Colin surprised them by smiling at Addy and Adam. "I shall see that our staff is mindful that we now have a little one in the house, though I know Mrs. Pritchard and Cook are already planning and sharing ideas for ways to tempt Master Adam's sweet tooth."

"Thank you, Colin." Addy turned to Edmund, and a feeling of rightness filled her at the sight of Adam leaning against his chest.

How long would it take Edmund to realize a child's love truly was magical?

Chapter Fourteen

Addy preceded Edmund and Adam into the library and was introduced to the captain—who looked more like a pirate, sporting a black eyepatch and matching sling—and Mr. King, who led a group of the famed red-coated Runners. Unsure of why they were asked to attend the meeting, she stood at Edmund's side until the viscount motioned for her to be seated.

Choosing one of the leather wing-back chairs by the warmth of the fire, she was not surprised when Edmund walked over and handed Adam to her. "He'll be more comfortable if you are holding him when my brother raises his voice."

She started to ask why, then realized his brother had raised his voice more than once, though not in anger, merely as his customary volume of speaking. She brushed the dark waves out of Adam's eyes and waited to hear what this meeting was about.

King stared at Edmund, but it was Coventry who asked if he'd walked into a wall. Colin's chuckle had her realizing that while she had grown accustomed to seeing the bruises on Edmund's face since their first meeting at the Lyon's Den, the other two gentlemen had not seen his battered features.

"It's a story best left for another time," Edmund said. "May I ask why you need to see both myself and my intended?"

Coventry nodded to Edmund. "Congratulations." He turned and smiled at Addy. "I take it you are widowed, Mrs. Fernside?"

Colin grunted. "Admit your information is wrong and get to the point without dancing around it, Coventry."

Addy noted the way the captain's one green eye glittered with emotion. He was obviously irritated about something. She was surprised when he looked her way and met her gaze. "Our information was indeed correct. Mrs. Fernside was the woman identified leaving Templeton House over a year ago. More than one of your servants gave vivid descriptions."

Addy's heart lodged in her throat. *They knew?*

King chose that moment to speak. "Though it is true that we tracked Mrs. Fernside to her home in Leeds—"

Addy was relieved to know the connection with the strangers was one her husband-to-be trusted. "You were the ones asking questions about my sister?"

"Ah yes…your *sister*," King said. "She was the missing element that we were unaware of. Forgive me, Mrs. Fernside, for assuming you were the actress involved with Adam Broadbank."

"I have never felt called to spout lines and sing in front of an audience the way my younger sister has," she said. Feeling the need to state her innocence, she told the men, "I have never, nor would I ever, engaged in an illicit affair. I am appalled that you would think that of me."

Coventry said, "Forgive me—I was relying on what we thought to be the entirety of the information we required to uncover the mystery."

King cleared his throat. "As to that, Mrs. Fernside, I must clarify my part. The men sent to Leeds are two of my men. I assure you they would never attempt to break into anyone's home"—he paused—

"unless it was a dire situation, and someone was being held against their will—or a disaster."

"Disaster?" Addy asked.

"Fire," King replied.

"Thank you, gentlemen. I accept your apologies. Now, if you will excuse me."

She rose, settling Adam on her hip, but before she could leave, Coventry stopped her. "We are not quite through, Mrs. Fernside."

She hesitated, unsure of what more they could possibly want to know about her lack of control over her sister's choices. "What more do you need?"

"We need you to tell us all you can remember about the attempted break-in," King told her. "It would seem someone else is highly interested in your connection to the former viscount's heir."

"And your nephew," Coventry added.

Addy all but collapsed into the chair she'd just vacated. "What could anyone possibly want to know about Adam?"

"That, Mrs. Fernside, is what we hope to uncover—with your assistance."

For the next forty-five minutes, she answered a barrage of questions, most mundane and seemingly unimportant, but a few had her stomach churning with anxiety. Specifically, if she'd entertained any gentlemen at Thorne House, if she had an understanding with any one gentleman, and if she had ever been to the Theatre Royal Covent Garden.

AFTER ADDY RESPONDED no to those last three questions more than once, Edmund shot to his feet. "You are finished interrogating my intended." He offered his hand and drew Addy to her feet. After taking the sleepy boy in one arm, he offered the other to Addy.

He did not bother to bid the men goodbye. He was too irritated to speak to either of them. Though he doubted Colin had agreed to the line of questioning ahead of time, his brother hadn't stopped the repeated inquiries.

Halfway to the foot of the stairs, Addy stumbled. One of the footmen rushed to her side, offering his assistance. Hanson sent the other to fetch Mrs. Pritchard.

The housekeeper arrived a few minutes later. "Now then, you're overtired, you poor thing. Edmund, if you'll lead the way, I'll see to Mrs. Fernside." He was about to protest when Mrs. Pritchard added, "We'll be right behind you."

A few minutes later, he was being escorted from her bedchamber with the reassurance they would send for him if he was needed.

He marveled at how quickly Addy had recovered her equilibrium and was changing Adam, getting him ready for bed. He thanked Mrs. Pritchard, knowing she had been the one to think of locating the heirloom crib Adam would be sleeping in. *Pretty soon, Colin and Gemma will be needing the crib for their babe.* He wondered if his brother had asked Gemma outright if she was expecting, or if he was waiting for her to blurt out her news.

Having carried Adam up the stairs, Edmund found his job was apparently finished for the evening. Time to go find out what in the bloody hell Coventry and King had been thinking with their intense questioning of Addy.

Without knocking, he opened the library door and stalked inside.

"Ah, there you are, Edmund," Coventry said.

"We were just about to have Hanson find you," his brother added.

King looked to Colin and then Coventry. "There is a situation that has arisen that you need to be made aware of."

Edmund paused mid-step. Warily, he asked, "Does it involve my intended or nephew?" When no one answered right away, he said, "Don't dance around it! Tell me what I need to know."

King nodded to Colin, who explained, "I received a missive while you were out. The contents had me consulting with King and Coventry."

"Obviously it has you worried," Edmund replied. "How can I help?"

Coventry said, "By remaining impartial and letting us do what we do best."

Be damned! "Are you asking me, or warning me not to take sides?"

"Your brother is cognizant of the fact that my men are well equipped to handle these types of situations."

"I will not agree unless I know the contents of the missive you received, Colin."

His brother inhaled deeply. "I knew you were going to be difficult."

"A Broadbank trait," Edmund replied. "You are wasting time by not confiding in me."

"Tell him," Coventry urged.

"The missive asked for five thousand pounds to remain silent on the matter of a certain actress and our brother."

Edmund's heart raced. "I see. When does this nameless person expect to be paid?"

King said, "Tonight."

Edmund gritted his teeth. "Where?"

"Vauxhall Gardens," Coventry replied.

"Ah, the Dark Walk." Edmund had heard rumors of those accosted on the infamous unlit walk at the back of the pleasure gardens. "I'll deliver the coin. You have too much to lose if you go and are coshed on the back of the head by some thug."

"We Broadbanks are known for having hard heads," Colin said.

Edmund's snort of laughter eased the tension in the room. "Aye, which is why you will see the rightness of my going. Do you really want the second in line to the viscountcy to end up fatherless as well?"

"What's this?" Coventry asked.

"Second in line, behind yourself?" King inquired.

"Best tell them, Colin. Is there anything else I need to know? Any instructions?" Edmund asked.

"Aye, but since you are not going, you do not need to know," Colin replied.

"The hell I don't!"

Coventry intervened. "Tell him—he has a right to know."

Colin glared at his brother. "Follow the Druid's Walk to where it ends at the Dark Walk. Look for a one-legged man on crutches who answers to the name of Smith. Hand him the bag of coin."

"What's to stop the bastards from demanding more coin the moment they spend what I give them tonight?" Edmund asked.

"My men," King replied.

"My men," Coventry stated at the same time.

Before any further discussion could take place, Edmund said, "I'll be leaving as soon as I retrieve my pistol. I'm going to need more than a blade in case things get a bit sticky."

"Edmund—" the viscount began.

"Trust me," Edmund said over his shoulder as he quit the room. He could hear the rumble of their voices as they conferred with one another. They should argue for a bit longer, giving him time to arm himself.

THE THREE MEN watched Edmund stride from the room, then Coventry walked over to close the door. "I'll assign a man to follow your brother."

"I have men stationed along the interior perimeter of the pleasure garden—near Hermit's Walk and Druid's Lane...and the Dark Walk," King added.

"What of the exterior perimeter on Kennington Lane, and Loney's Lane?" the viscount asked.

King inclined his head. "You and Edmund resemble one another, and along the unlit walk, no one will be the wiser that it is not the viscount making the delivery."

Coventry agreed. "I have three other men I trust implicitly. I'll send them as well."

The viscount shook his head. "I feel it is my duty to go."

"No one would question your duty, especially after you make the announcement about your viscountess," Coventry assured him.

"As her husband—"

"You want to be the one to protect her from all harm," King finished for him. "Understood. However, you need to be *alive* in order to protect her."

"And your unborn child," Coventry added.

"We have not made an official announcement," Colin reminded him.

"I am not in the habit of repeating gossip," King replied, "which, at the moment, I assume this is."

The viscount grumbled, "Thank you." With a deep sigh, he reluctantly agreed. "See that my brother returns home to his intended—and our nephew—in one piece."

"That will not be a problem," King assured him.

"He may end up with a few more bruises," Coventry added.

Colin snorted. "I would expect no less from my brother. See to it he does not come home with any unwanted *gifts*."

"Gifts?" King asked.

"A lead ball in his back or shoulder."

The men quickly agreed and formed the rest of their plans, before sending for Perkins.

"Watch your backs," the viscount warned them.

"Watch yours," King replied.

Colin escorted the men to the door with the promise to send word if Edmund did not return by midnight.

"Bloody hell, I should be the one to handle this," he said after they left.

"Handle what, my love?"

He turned at the softly murmured question and held out his hand. Gemma grasped it. Her unspoken worry shot through him. "Nothing of import, lass."

She frowned but did not contradict him.

Pleased, he pulled her into his arms and breathed deeply, soothed by the familiar scent of lavender. "How are you feeling after a brief rest?"

"Tired, though I should not be."

He pressed a kiss to her forehead and another to the tip of her nose. "Did you forget the physician's warning to expect to be exhausted for the first few months?"

She settled against him. "I was hoping he would be wrong."

He swallowed his laughter, not wanting to take the chance he would offend her tender sensibilities. That too was something the physician had warned him about. The list of things to expect and what could go wrong had been daunting.

His brother was right—Colin's place was here with Gemma and their unborn babe. He'd have to thank Edmund later.

Chapter Fifteen

Edmund did not waste any time, nor did he bother to enlighten his brother as to his plans. *Bloody know-it-all!* He loaded the pistol he'd acquired after that madman broke into Templeton House a year ago. Next, he opened the pouches containing powder, lead balls, and wadding. Satisfied he had sufficient ammunition, he stuffed the leather pouches in the pockets of his greatcoat.

Colin's oft-repeated warning echoed in his head—best to carry a knife in your boot when venturing into London's seamier side. He smiled, and did not need to check; he'd been carrying a blade since he was accosted by a footpad a few years back.

Armed, expecting trouble, he slipped out of his bedchamber and walked to the servants' staircase at the other end of the hallway. He knew his whereabouts would be reported to his brother no matter if he exited their house using the front door or the servants' door…in fact, he counted on it.

Nodding to the footman and two maids heading toward him, he headed to the rear of the house. He opened the door and was met with resistance.

"Expected you a bit ago," Perkins remarked.

Edmund moved to step around the retired sailor, but the man anticipated him and blocked his path.

"Tell my brother he wins," Edmund said. "You tried to stop me. Now step aside, Perkins."

The older man shook his head. "I take orders from the captain, not you."

"I'm on a mission to avenge the woman I am marrying tomorrow. You can join me, or face my wrath."

Perkins stared at him for a moment before saying, "The captain didn't expect you to disobey orders."

Edmund chuckled. "Ah, my brother's only fault."

Perkins did not agree or disagree. "I've never served under a better man than Captain Broadbank."

"My brother can be overbearing, obstinate, and hardheaded...then again, so can I. It's a trait we Broadbanks carry," Edmund said. "Now then, you can either go hand to hand with me or let me pass. I am certain I'm not the only one armed to the teeth."

Perkins' face lost all expression, and Edmund knew he would earn a few more bruises before the night was over if he tangled with the wiry seaman.

"Or...you could ask Grant to cover your position and lend a hand. I have a feeling I may need backup where I'm headed."

The man didn't waste any time. He whistled loudly. A few moments later, Grant materialized out of the dark. Glancing from Perkins to Edmund, he asked, "Is there a problem?"

"Tell the captain not to worry. I've got his brother's back." Perkins paused, then added, "Have one of the other lads cover your position."

Grant agreed and surprised Edmund by cupping his hands by his mouth and imitating a bird call.

The faint answering call seemed to satisfy Perkins, who turned and grinned at him. "Where are we off to?"

Edmund noted the seaman matched his pace as he strode quickly toward the entrance to the alley. "The Dark Walk."

"We might have a bit of fun tonight after all."

Lifting his hand to hail a hackney, he glanced over his shoulder. The wry grin on Perkins' face had him shaking his head. "I can handle this without you."

"But I'd miss all the fun." Perkins sounded like a child denied his Christmas pudding.

Edmund suppressed a chuckle. He nodded to the driver and relayed their destination, Vauxhall Gardens. He climbed into the cab, not surprised when Perkins proceeded to check his pockets. Edmund had expected to see the leather pouch of powder, another containing lead balls, and even the two wicked blades did not shock him…but the lengths of rope did.

"Are you expecting to tie someone up?"

The sailor grinned. "Always a high point of my day when I can."

Edmund snorted with laughter. "Good to know, Perkins."

THE DRIVER SLOWED to a stop, and the men alighted. "Coventry and King are bound to have a few men stationed nearby," Edmund told Perkins. "I do not plan to rely on their help."

"I'd be wary of well-dressed gents feigning a sudden weakness, or a cry for help once we reach the Dark Walk."

"Fool me once…" Edmund muttered.

"Captain told me what happened."

Edmund wasn't surprised. His brother had rung a peal over his head when he found out what happened while he was away at sea. "Did Colin tell you he insisted I carry a blade in my boot?"

Perkins shrugged. "Man's got a right to arm himself when there's trouble afoot." He slowed his steps. "Mind that one," he rasped with a nod toward the man stumbling toward them.

Confident in his ability, Edmund squared his shoulders. "I can take him."

Perkins placed a hand on his arm. "Aye, but you have more important business elsewhere."

"True."

The man stopped a few feet in front of them, swaying. Expecting trouble, Edmund watched the man's eyes narrow as he and Perkins drew closer. Instead of offering help, they walked past the fellow.

Edmund sensed the interloper's movement a heartbeat before Perkins swung around and had his blade to the bigger man's throat. "We're not looking for trouble this night, mind?"

The shocked expression would be worth the telling later, but it was the man's reaction to Perkins patting him on the shoulder as the blade was withdrawn that spoke volumes. Colin's man wasn't willing to *start* a fight, but Edmund would bet his life that the would-be attacker knew Perkins would finish one. The man held up his hands and walked away.

They walked past shrubs lining the walkway and heard muffled sounds of lovers engaging in a tryst. Out of the corner of his eye, Edmund noted a man standing alone. As they approached, he pulled a pocket watch from his waistcoat, glanced at it, and put it away.

Edmund could not explain why he did not suspect the man of shady business, but as they passed, the gent gave a slight shake of his head before retreating into the shadows.

Twice more it happened.

"Good to know Captain Coventry and King's men are on the job," Perkins remarked. "What's your plan?"

Edmund pitched his voice low. "After I hand over the coin to the one-legged man, we each grab an arm and drag him back to Templeton House."

Perkins shook his head. "What about the two other blokes waiting out of sight?"

"Two?"

"At least," he replied.

Edmund stopped in his tracks. "Wait here!"

Perkins grabbed him by the arm. "What are you about?"

Edmund growled, "Evening the odds."

The older man let go. "Find out who he works for first!"

Not the worst idea the seaman had offered.

A man turned to face Edmund as he approached. Though the path was lit, the areas in between the torches were dark.

"Help you?" the man rasped.

"Did King send you or Coventry?"

The man paused, and for a moment Edmund wondered if he'd guessed wrong until the man replied, "King."

"Perkins and I need your help with the rest of our plan. What's your name?"

"Thompson."

"I'm—"

"The viscount's brother Edmund."

"My plan is to grab our one-legged blackmailer and drag him back to Templeton House with us."

Thompson squared his shoulders. "I've been known to take on two or three men at a time."

"And arise the victor?" Edmund asked.

The other man answered, "Aye."

"Perkins has rope."

Thompson snorted. "Not a surprise—he's a former sailor. I keep a gag handy."

Edmund was impressed. "I only thought to bring a pistol, ammunition, and two blades."

Thompson grinned. "I didn't think I'd be getting in on the action tonight."

Edmund wondered if all of Coventry and King's men enjoyed brawling. In their line of work, they probably did.

They met up with Perkins and entered the Dark Walk, only to find it empty. "What now?" Edmund asked.

"We wait," Perkins replied.

They didn't have to wait long before an odd sound reached them. It sounded like a partial footfall, and then what sounded like a cane—no…two canes. Anticipation burst through Edmund.

Perkins' hand on his shoulder kept Edmund from giving away their plan by moving closer. At the moment, all they could see was darkness, but what they heard was their quarry moving closer. If they couldn't see him, he could not see them.

A rustling on the other side of the hedge had the men flanking Edmund. He could feel the tension radiating from them. Excellent—the three of them were ready to spring into action!

A voice nearby rasped, "The coin is the first step in Honeywell's plan."

A deeper voice replied, "He's right—taking down the house of Moreland is child's play."

Edmund could feel the bite of Perkins' and Thompson's fingers on his shoulders keeping him from striking out at the two men waiting to enact their plans. The bleeding bastards had no idea his brother had already outsmarted them.

Perkins pulled a knife from his boot and motioned for them to wait.

Anger and frustration pulsed through Edmund's veins until he saw red. Drawing in a breath to clear his vision, he did as he was told.

The sound of two moans had him silently applauding Perkins' stealth and proficiency with a blade. The sailor reappeared just as a voice called out, "Moreland?"

"Aye," Edmund replied.

"Do ye have the coin?"

"I would be stupid to be waiting for you on the Dark Walk if I did not."

The snicker sounded close. "Toss it here."

"I cannot throw it that far. Come closer."

The man demanded, "Where's the coin?"

Edmund's answer was a right cross.

The man wobbled but didn't fall. Thompson held him while Perkins bound his hands to his crutches and tied another length of rope around the man's neck before handing it to Edmund.

"Black Sam! Horrington!"

The one-legged man's cries went unanswered as Thompson pulled a gag from his pocket.

The man stopped fighting, his gaze fixed on Edmund. "Who in the bloody hell are you?"

"Edmund Broadbank." When the one-legged man didn't react, Edmund added, "Viscount Moreland's brother."

Thompson tied the gag around the man's mouth. "Save the rest for when we get to Bow Street."

"Thank you for your assistance, Thompson," Edmund said.

"My pleasure. King will be well pleased tonight." Turning to Perkins, Thompson asked, "Need a hand with the thugs in the bushes?"

"Aye," Perkins replied. "Edmund, if you'll follow along with your prisoner, they're right behind the hedge."

"Why don't you bring the men out here?"

Perkins shook his head, ignoring Edmund's question. "Thompson, you grab one thug. I'll grab the other. Edmund can lead this one by tugging on the rope." When Edmund didn't move fast enough, Perkins added, "We'll use their carriage to haul them to Bow Street."

"Better than my plan to haul them back along the Druid's Walk through the entrance," Edmund replied.

Thompson snickered as he hoisted one man over his shoulder.

"King is going to be very pleased."

Perkins followed suit, drawing his weapon as they stealthily approached Kennington Lane, expecting a guard to be waiting by the carriage.

"Guess they thought the viscount would come alone," Thompson remarked.

Perkins motioned for Thompson to lean his prisoner against the wheel of the carriage, then nodded to Edmund. "Steady him so he doesn't fall on his face—he'll be less recognizable."

Thompson climbed into the carriage and helped pull the man inside. After leaning him in one corner, he turned around and reached for the second prisoner. "Help me check them for weapons, Perkins."

Edmund waited, keeping a sharp eye on his prisoner. "Were you injured serving His Majesty?"

The man ignored the question.

Edmund realized answering was impossible with the gag. "If you promise not to call for help, I'll remove the gag."

The man nodded, and Edmund did as he'd said.

"Lost my leg in the Peninsular War at Rolica."

"My brother served in the Royal Navy, captained the *HMS Britannia*. He had to retire when our eldest brother Adam died of a virulent fever, leaving the viscountcy vacant."

"I nearly died from blood loss and then infection."

"I know more about the battles at sea because of Colin. Thank you for defending the Crown and our country. What is your name?"

"Redfern."

"Hand him over," Perkins said.

Edmund leaned into the carriage and announced, "I'm removing the rope around his neck. Redfern here lost his leg in the Peninsular Wars."

Perkins pushed Edmund out of the way, quickly loosened the knot, and lifted the rope from around Redfern's neck. "Which battle?"

"Rolica," Redfern replied.

Perkins met his gaze, then said, "War is hell, Redfern." He and Edmund handed the man inside the carriage.

Edmund sensed they would both be speaking on behalf of the former soldier, asking for leniency. The other two thugs—and their apparent employer, Honeywell—were another matter altogether. He would leave them to flounder on their own. His conscience would not let the embattled war hero suffer any longer on his own.

He would speak to Colin. Between them, they would find a place where Redfern could gain some of his former confidence back—how else would the man have managed in one of the king's regiments?

His gaze met Perkins'. When the other man gave a quick nod, Edmund sensed they were of the same mind. They would speak to King when they arrived at Bow Street, and mayhap Coventry before approaching Colin.

Pleased with the way the evening had transpired, Edmund let his mind drift to thoughts of the wedding that would take place hours from now. Sealing their vows with a kiss was the first step toward wooing his bride-to-be. Convincing her to consummate their union immediately after they said their vows may take a bit more persuasion. It would be for their nephew's protection—and her own, given that a blackmailer had somehow entered into their lives. Careful planning was called for.

He loved nothing better than deciding on a plan of action and moving forward.

Chapter Sixteen

Adam's muffled cries woke Addy before dawn. Rising to see if he needed a change or just to be soothed back to sleep, she was hopeful it was the latter.

He rolled over, and the tears in his eyes clutched at her heart.

"There now, little one," she crooned as she lifted him into her arms. "I'm here." He sighed, grabbed the braid slung over her shoulder, and brushed it against his face. "You are so silly. Doesn't that tickle?"

He put his thumb in his mouth, brushing the tip of her braid against the end of his nose as she settled him in his crib and changed his damp nappies and sleeping gown.

When he was dry, she tried to put him down, but he started to fuss. "Don't wake the household, Adam. We don't want to wear out our welcome, do we?"

He stared at her with those entrancing, deep gray eyes, and she knew he would not be going back to sleep without a few sips of warm milk.

"If you promise to be quiet, we can sneak down to the kitchen for that milk." He pulled his thumb out of his mouth and nodded. "One loud peep and it's back to bed without a drink." Adam smiled his adorable baby smile, and her heart melted. "Fine, then—if you make a peep, no biscuit."

He giggled at the word. He may not understand everything said to him, but he knew the words *milk* and *biscuit*.

She donned her dressing gown and tied the belt into a bow, so Adam wouldn't pull it free, as he had during their last early-morning excursion to find milk and a snack. After wrapping a blanket around him, she put her finger to her lips, their signal for him to be quiet as a mouse. He mimicked the movement.

Thankful every other sconce had a candle burning brightly, she was able to make her way along the hallway to the servants' staircase. It was too dark to close the door behind her, so she left it open to shed a bit of light on the steps. Adam didn't start squirming until they reached the bottom.

Surprised to hear sounds in the kitchen, she turned around, and would have bumped into the viscount if he hadn't reached out to steady her.

"What are you doing up, Mrs. Fernside?"

She brushed the tips of her fingers over Adam's wavy, dark hair and told him, "Someone wanted to rise before the sun. We were hoping to find a bit of milk to warm up, and maybe a bit of bread or scone."

He motioned for her to precede him. "This way."

"Do you normally rise before dawn, your lordship?"

He shook his head. "Extenuating circumstances."

"Anything I can help with?"

"Why don't you see to Adam's needs first? I'll come back to fetch you."

She wondered at his cryptic response but did not question him. He reached past her and opened the kitchen door, greeted the cook, and told the woman to take good care of her and Adam.

After Adam had finished his cup and eaten half a scone, his eyes drifted closed. Contentment filled her as he fell asleep in her arms.

She had never thought to marry, let alone become a mother. Circumstances, and a much higher power, had made the choice for her.

As she pressed a kiss to the top of Adam's head, she knew she would not change a thing. Now, if only she could get to know her husband-to-be better, she would be assured that they would be able to settle into a routine that would be amenable to the both of them.

She hoped it would not mean they maintained separate lives while living under the same roof. The way he'd held her gaze, and kissed her hand, led her to believe he may be attracted to her. Hope filled her, but she was afraid to ask. Could she live with a marriage where the spouses rarely spoke and saw one another a few times a year? If she had to, she would have no choice but to accept it.

"Thank you for the milk and scones, Cook." She paused and held the older woman's gaze. "I know this may sound strange, but it doesn't feel quite right calling you by your occupation."

The woman's smile had Addy smiling in return.

"It was easier just to respond when the earl began calling me Cook instead of my name."

"What is your name?"

"Dorothy."

"What a lovely name. Do you mind if I call you Dorothy? You can call me Addy. It's much easier than Adelaide."

"That would be just fine, Addy, and your little one's name is Adam?"

"He's actually my nephew. He was so young when my sister gave him into my care, but I plan to tell him all about Lily. It wouldn't be right that he should not know his true mother."

Dorothy placed a hand on Addy's shoulder and patted it. "From what I've observed this morning, you didn't balk at bringing Adam down to have his cup of milk and something to eat. You coddled and cuddled him. You are a wonderful mother."

Warmth spread up from Addy's toes. "Thank you. I do worry that I will do something wrong that will scar him for life."

"All mothers worry—it's a sign that you care. Why don't you take that little angel upstairs and put him back to bed? He's almost asleep."

"Thank you, Dorothy. I think I will. If the viscount is looking for me, please tell him I'm going to put Adam to bed."

Mindful that the servants were now bustling about with their first tasks of the day, Addy used the servants' door that opened into the entryway. She'd rather not be seen in her dressing gown and nightrail, but knew that at this hour of the day she would hamper the staff's ability to go about their duties using their staircase. She was covered from her chin to her toes, she reasoned, so it should be fine.

Hanson was speaking with two footmen when she opened the door. He paused to ask, "Is there something you need, Mrs. Fernside?"

"No, thank you. Adam wanted his early-morning cup of milk."

"Ah, shall I escort you to your bedchamber?"

"No thank you, we'll be fine."

"His lordship would hang me from the yardarm...er chandelier, if I did not at least walk with you to ensure you did not trip going up the stairs with Master Adam in your arms."

"Yardarm?"

"Ah...chandelier," he reminded her. "It's the closest we have to a ship's yardarm."

Her empty stomach churned at the very idea. "He wouldn't really hang you...would he?"

Hanson lifted his chin as he accompanied her. "I have no desire to find out."

She met his steady gaze and knew she would never want to be the reason the viscount carried out that threat. "I'm happy for your assistance, Hanson," she said. "Thank you."

He opened the bedchamber door for her and stood back so she

could enter the room. "I shall see you in a few hours."

"Would it be too early if I requested breakfast in an hour or so?"

"Not at all. His lordship and Mr. Broadbank usually breakfast at six o'clock on the dot."

"I would not dream of interrupting them, as Adam will no doubt only nap for half an hour or so."

"Shall I ask Cook to prepare a tray for you?"

Addy hated to ask for favors—however, she could not expect Adam to be left in a maid's care while she ate with the viscount and her husband-to-be. "If it would not be too much trouble."

"Not at all. I shall speak with her at once."

"Thank you, Hanson."

"My pleasure, Mrs. Fernside."

She hid the wince she felt every time anyone addressed her as *Mrs.* It couldn't be helped and was essential to guarding Adam's identity. She had a bad feeling that King and Captain Coventry's arrival had more to do with her nephew than herself.

After brushing a kiss to his brow, she put him to bed. The knock on her door surprised her, and had Adam squirming. She rushed to open it, so whoever it was did not knock louder and wake him.

"I just put Adam down," she explained to the maid. "Thank you for the hot water. I was about to get ready for the day."

"I'm to offer my assistance, Mrs. Fernside. My name's Maisy."

"Thank you, Maisy. I can manage for now. Adam's been up for an hour already, and he tends to be cranky if he doesn't get another nap in before he rises for the day."

Maisy smiled as she peered down at the little boy. "He has the sweetest smile. You are so fortunate he sleeps for you."

"So I've been told." A glance had Addy estimating the maid's age to be nearly ten and eight. "Have you had the care of many infants?"

Maisy nodded. "I have half a dozen younger brothers and sisters and helped me mum watch them until I was hired by the earl."

"In that case, I'd be most grateful for your assistance, since you have experience. It's not that I do not willingly trust others—I'm still so new at being a mother. I'm often feeling out of my element."

Maisy's warm expression eased the worst of Addy's fears. "Why don't I set out a gown for you while you make use of the hot water?"

"Thank you, Maisy."

The maid was mumbling beneath her breath, and Addy had a feeling it was the limited selection of gowns. There were a number of more important expenses she had to take care of—namely the staff, the tenant farmers, and Adam. She did the best she could with serviceable used gowns the local seamstress sold at a reduced price, while Lily never wore a gown unless it had been created exclusively for her. Addy had never minded all that much—that was, until now. She hoped her limited wardrobe did not embarrass Edmund.

"How about the deep blue gown? Your eyes will positively gleam. Such an unusual color, my lady."

Addy chuckled. "I'm not a lady...well that is to say, not a titled lady, though I was brought up to be." The maid seemed to digest that information. Before she could ask any other questions, Addy offered, "My sister shares the same eye color, though her hair is black as a raven's wing, while mine is light brown."

"Honey blonde, I'd say, Mrs. Fernside."

She paused in her ablutions and stared into the looking glass hanging above the washstand. "Would you?" Mayhap in the sunlight it would appear more blonde than brown. "My sister often commented on the nondescript color of my hair."

"I have two younger sisters with a similar shade of hair. It glistens with blonde highlights in the sunshine and always reminds Mum of honey."

"Thank you for mentioning it, Maisy." Addy dried her face and hands. "Father had the same hair color, and his always gleamed whenever we were outside."

"There you have it, Mrs. Fernside. After I help you dress, I can put your hair up for you."

Addy smiled at the younger woman. "You'll spoil me with all of the attention. I can manage, but thank you for the offer."

Adam started to fuss, and before she could pick him up, Maisy was there smiling and cooing to him as he opened his eyes. "Such beautiful eyes. They are quite like his lordship's...and Mr. Broadbank's."

Addy was surprised, yet encouraged, when Adam reached for Maisy's face to pat it. "He's quite taken with you, Maisy. He does not take to strangers."

"Mum remarked how much she'd miss my helping with my brothers and sisters once I signed on to work for his lordship."

Adam squealed with delight as Maisy rubbed his button nose with hers.

Relief filled Addy. "He's taken with you."

"Like I said, I'm used to taking care of little ones. Mum says I have the heart for it."

"Your mother is right. Have you considered becoming a nanny instead of a lady's maid?"

"I have, but I would never turn my back on his lordship—he offered me a job when I was desperate to find one. Mum depends on my pay to help feed my brothers and sisters."

"I know what that is like. I had to care for my younger sister after we lost our parents. It is not easy to step into that role."

Maisy agreed as she hugged Adam and dressed him for the day. When he tried to run to the door, she deftly swept him into her arms. "You must wait for your mum to be ready, Master Adam."

It was a strange but marvelous feeling to know that Lily's little one trusted three people in his life: Addy, Maisy, and Edmund.

"I'll be ready in a trice," Addy promised him. She turned her back to her maid to do up her buttons.

Maisy stepped back and smiled. "You look lovely, Mrs. Fernside."

Are you certain you do not want my help with your hair?"

"It takes me but a moment." True to her words, Addy swept her hair behind her shoulders, scooped it up, twisted it, and added a few hairpins. A few strands slipped free from the pins, but she did not have time to worry about them. She needed to see that she and Adam were fed and ready for whenever Mr. Broadbank sent for them. No matter what he asked of her, she would be accommodating. Addy did wonder what he would look like once his facial injuries healed—even more handsome than he already appeared!

The knock on the door had her setting those thoughts aside to concentrate on the present. "Come in."

Mrs. Pritchard smiled as she entered the bedchamber. "Wonderful to see that you and Master Adam are awake and ready for the day. Mr. Broadbank requests that you join him for breakfast."

She hesitated, not wishing to cause friction on her first day at Templeton House, but her nephew's needs came first. "I have not had a chance to feed Adam yet. He's quite adept at feeding himself," she remarked, "but he does make an awful mess."

The housekeeper's eyes twinkled. "As would any little one the same age. Shall I ask Mr. Broadbank if he would mind waiting until after Adam eats?"

Addy's heart slowed at the housekeeper's kind suggestion. "If it would not be too much trouble. You see, he's had so much upheaval for one so young. I try to keep to a routine." Worry coursed through her as she remembered it took longer than normal for him to fall asleep. "He didn't bother anyone while he settled down to sleep last night, did he?"

"Not at all, Mrs. Fernside. I shall speak with Mr. Broadbank and then see that Cook sends up Adam's breakfast."

"Thank you so much, Mrs. Pritchard. I promise to keep my special requests for Adam to a minimum."

"No need. Cook and I are quite happy to help however we can. I'll have that tray sent up." The housekeeper turned to the maid, instructing, "If you have finished assisting Mrs. Fernside and Master Adam, the viscountess wishes to speak with you."

"Is there anything else you need, Mrs. Fernside?" Maisy asked.

"No thank you," Addy replied. "You've been a wonderful help this morning, Maisy."

The maid handed the little boy to Addy and swiftly left the bedchamber.

"I am happy to hear that you are pleased with Maisy," Mrs. Pritchard said. "She has only been with the staff for a little over a year but has made herself quite indispensable in that time. We had no idea she was so adept at taking care of children."

Someone knocked on the door. "Come in," Addy called.

"Ah, Mrs. Pritchard, thought I might find you here," Edmund said, entering.

"Mr. Broadbank, was there something you needed?" the housekeeper asked.

Addy stared at the man she'd promised to wed and felt her breath hitch in her lungs. He stepped into the room, and a ray of earlymorning sunlight highlighted his rugged features. Though the bruises were still evident, more of the swelling had receded.

His deep chuckle brought her back to her senses. "Forgive me—it was an early morning, Mr. Broadbank," she said.

Edmund's beautifully sculpted lips lifted on one side. His crooked smile went right to her heart. Unable to think of a thing to say, she echoed his smile, and she nearly swallowed her tongue at the depth of emotion swirling in his wintry eyes. It was intense, but at the same time compelling.

"Is there something you needed, Mr. Broadbank?"

Mrs. Pritchard's question had Adam squirming in her arms, reaching for Edmund. Taking the little boy from Addy, he responded, "I came to invite Master Adam and Mrs. Fernside to join me at breakfast." Adam patted the side of his face and leaned against him. "It would seem our nephew is quite content to join me. Won't you?"

Addy's heart lodged in her throat while heat pulsed through her veins. Her nephew had taken to Edmund from the first, and Edmund accepted Adam as the heir to the viscountcy. They would marry tonight. She hoped to be able to look the other way while Edmund continued with his life, all the while pretending their marriage was more than an arrangement for Adam's protection—and that of the viscountcy. Though it was not what she had hoped for in her youthful dreams of marriage one day, it would be all right.

STARING INTO EYES the color of the seas his brother had described to him years ago, Edmund was entranced by the confusion, embarrassment, and more...the *hope* in Addy's gaze. "Please join us, Adelaide."

Hand to her throat, she gathered herself while he watched. Admiration filled him. He was confident that this woman would rally in the face of whatever life tossed in her path. Had she not already done so, taking on the care of her sister's babe?

"I must warn you, Adam insists on feeding himself, and he'll—"

"Be fine," Edmund interrupted. Noticing the worry in the depths of her gaze, he sought to soothe it. "If you like, we can eat in the anteroom behind the pantry."

The gasp had them both turning to face Mrs. Pritchard. "That room is not fit for company. It is for messengers...and his lordship's men."

"It shall suit our purposes for this morning, Mrs. Pritchard. Please inform Cook. We shall be down momentarily."

The housekeeper inclined her head and left to do his bidding.

Addy's lighthearted chuckle wrapped around his heart. "You did not let me answer," she said.

"I did not want to waste the time. I have a feeling young Adam is anxious to eat, aren't you, lad?"

"Eat!"

Adam's joyful reply had him grinning. His brother's heir had been found. Edmund would marry Addy this evening, affording her and Adam the protection of his name and that of the viscountcy.

And tonight, he would begin wooing his wife.

It was going to be all right.

Chapter Seventeen

"What in the devil are you doing back here?" the viscount said before he apologized to Addy. "Please forgive my brother for his lack of manners. Even I know this room is not fit for polite company, let alone a small boy."

Edmund's laughter rang out. "Stow it, Colin. I wanted to eat with my bride-to-be and our nephew. You have to agree, it would be frowned upon by our staff to allow a child to dine with us. Once Master Adam is ten and four… Mayhap, until then, they expect him to dine in the nursery." When his brother opened his mouth to speak, Edmund continued, "If that gets your smallclothes in a twist, it cannot be helped."

The gasp of shock, followed by the bellow of Colin's laughter, had Adam clapping his hands in delight.

"Forgive me, Addy," Edmund said. "I normally don't speak of such things in polite company; however, as we are to be married this evening, it's best you know the truth—"

Colin regained control enough to interrupt, "Neither one of us bows to convention. Especially in our own home."

Addy remarked, "So it would seem."

"Meaning?" the viscount grumbled.

Edmund's sigh was audible. "The volume of your voice, brother."

Adam chose that moment to toss the last bite of scone from his plate. It landed with a plop in Edmund's teacup, splashing the contents onto his waistcoat.

The viscount's rumble of laughter had Adam clapping again.

"Best have my valet see to your waistcoat. Tea stains."

"Bloody—"

Colin frowned at him. "Language."

Shock had Edmund's mouth hanging open for a moment before he closed it. "Apologies, Addy."

She was busy mopping up the mess Adam made, but apparently heard him. "I would not want you to think me a shrew, but I must insist you do not teach Adam your colorful expressions until he is much older."

"That should be an enlightening conversation between you and our nephew, brother," Colin said. "By the by, I need to speak to you about last night."

"Is everything all right?"

Edmund heard the edge of worry in her voice, and sought to distract her. "Nothing to worry about. Business matters between my brother and I—right, Colin?"

The viscount inclined his head. "I'll be waiting in the library. Shall I have my valet meet us there?"

Addy's hand on his arm distracted Edmund. The warmth of her small hand should not have surprised him, as he'd taken off his frockcoat at her request before they sat down to prevent Adam from accidentally spilling on it.

The heat spread from her palm through the thin layer of his cambric shirt, branding him. He lifted his gaze to find her staring at him. He could get lost for days in her siren's eyes. The more time spent in her company, the more he realized he wanted a lifetime with her.

"Edmund!"

He looked over his shoulder. "What?"

"I'll not stand for insubordination from my—"

Edmund rose to his feet, but instead of answering his brother shout for shout, he kept his voice even. "You're on land now, Colin."

The momentary confusion in his brother's eyes had him wishing that their lives had not been irrevocably changed by the virulent fever that took their elder brother's life. Colin would still be aboard his ship, content with his life as captain of the *HMS Britannia* in the Royal Navy.

"Excuse me." His sister-in-law's soft voice brought him back to the present. "Is everything all right? I thought we would be breakfasting in the dining room."

"Gemma, love," the viscount said as he walked toward his wife, "I thought you would sleep longer."

Gazing at her husband, she replied, "I woke up a short while ago and find myself famished."

Edmund smiled at the look of wonder on his brother's face as Colin slipped his arm about Gemma's waist. "You're not nauseated?" the viscount asked.

"Not a bit." She smiled at Adam. "I do hope you left a scone or two for me, little man."

"Scone!" Adam mimicked.

"I think you've had enough for the moment, sweet boy," Addy told him. "I am so sorry he splashed you with tea, but I did warn you…"

"I beg to differ, Adelaide," Edmund replied. "You said he usually made a mess when he ate."

"And he did," she retorted.

"Ah, but you neglected to warn me he would be tossing bits of his scone. With perfect aim, I might add, to land in my teacup."

Gemma's giggles had Edmund turning to look at his sister-in-law. She was glowing with health. "You look wonderful, Gemma," he said.

She beamed at him. "I feel wonderful. I must confess, I had not thought I would until after our babe is born."

"That is wonderful news," Addy remarked. "I remember my sister claiming she could barely keep down more than a crust of stale bread for the first few months."

"Er...yes..." the viscount managed. "Edmund, I believe we shall leave the ladies to their...discussion."

Gemma ignored her husband, reaching for Adam when he held out his arms to her.

"Deserting me already?" Edmund grumbled, though he smiled as he said it. Adam didn't bother to look back as he settled himself in Gemma's arms, playing with the necklace she wore.

"Adam," Addy warned. "Do not tug on her ladyship's necklace."

"Gemma," the viscountess corrected her. "We're to be sisters-in-law by nightfall, and I have so missed conversations with someone my own age." With a smile for her husband and brother-in-law, she added, "Though I do enjoy conversing with the men in my life."

Colin bent and placed a kiss to her forehead then told his brother, "Coventry is due to arrive shortly. Ladies." He bowed and strode from the room.

"Addy, Gemma, Master Adam." Edmund grinned, bowed, and followed after him.

EDMUND CLOSED THE library door behind him. "Have you received any other information?"

"No," Colin replied. "I was mulling over all that we discussed last night. You're certain you wish to help Redfern?"

"You need to meet him for yourself. Once you speak with him, you'll understand why I asked Coventry to do what he could for the man."

"Was he in the Royal Navy?"

Edmund shook his head. "The regiment who fought in the Peninsular War... He lost his leg at Rolica."

"I do not need to meet with Redfern to make my decision. I trust yours. I will ask Coventry to consider adding the soldier to those who are currently employed by him. Before you ask, I will be happy to speak with Redfern."

Edmund relaxed his stance. "I thought because of his being involved in Honeywell's blackmail scheme—"

"King did confirm this Honeywell is a highflyer. Always in dun territory. Spends more than his allowance, gambling though he hasn't the good sense to wager wisely."

"Is there a connection between him and our nephew?"

"Aye." Colin paused for a moment before launching into what King had informed him. "Honeywell is a baronet, and therefore not entitled to a seat in the House of Lords. There are many who are waiting for the minor lord to marry an heiress to recoup their losses."

Edmund shook his head. "I take it he owes more than just gaming debts?"

"The man also has a reputation for playing fast and loose with actresses and demireps. Shall I continue?"

"There's more?" The viscount paced in front of the fireplace until Edmund grumbled, "Just get it said."

Colin stopped, turned, and met his brother's gaze. "King and Coventry's sources have indicated that Honeywell is not above blackmail, extorting coin from the unsuspecting—"

"In other words, those without your lofty connections."

"Aye. He is the lowest of low... He preys on women. The direr their circumstances, the better."

"Have either Coventry or King spoken with Lily Lovecote?"

"The two have been in close contact. Coventry elected King to speak with Miss Lovecote, believing his appearance may be too much of a shock for her to answer any questions."

"What is our next move?"

The viscount slowly smiled. "You and Mrs. Fernside are to be married."

Edmund frowned. "You know that is not what I mean. What are your plans? Have you already dispatched Perkins and Grant to spy on this Honeywell?"

"You know me too well."

"Bloody hell, Colin! Just tell me what you've planned and if Perkins or Grant—or both—have been sent to spy on the baronet."

"My plans are dependent upon what information Perkins and Grant manage to extract from Honeywell and his cronies in the stews."

"I can meet with—" Colin was already shaking his head, irritating Edmund no end. "This is my intended we are speaking of."

His brother's expression darkened. "And our nephew…Adam's rightful heir."

"Damnation!"

"If we have any say in the matter, Honeywell will be damned." The viscount's gaze brightened. "At the very least, he will be charged with blackmailing a peer of the realm. We're not certain who his connections in the upper level of society are yet. We're waiting for the information."

Though Edmund did not like waiting, or being told what to do, he asked, "You'll let me know how I can help and when you receive reports back from Coventry and King?"

"You have my word."

"By the by, I sent word to Madame Beaudoine that my bride-to-be is in need of a gown."

Colin laughed. "Excellent notion. The modiste supplied a beautiful gown for Gemma last year on short notice."

"And ended up witness to a hostage situation," Edmund murmured.

"She surprised me by not fainting on the spot, and supplied a number of dresses on short notice for my wife. Her blasted father confiscated her trunks."

"Did you notice that we gravitate toward women of strength and beauty?"

Colin clapped a hand to Edmund's shoulder. "We Broadbank men have a long history of marrying women of uncommon beauty, intelligence, and fortitude."

"Well said. I'd best let my valet see what he can do with my waistcoat." Edmund was halfway to the door when he asked, "You are certain that my marrying Miss Lovecote's sister is not a problem for you or Gemma?"

"Why in the bloody hell would it be?" the viscount demanded.

"Father is bound to have something to say. Given all that Addy has gone through in the last few days, I'd rather she did not have to listen to the earl posturing and making false assumptions as to how either you or I feel about being related to an actress by marriage."

"Leave Father to me."

Relieved, Edmund went in search of his intended.

Chapter Eighteen

Addy fingered the sheer blue green overlay between two fingers, marveling at the way it highlighted the cream-colored gown shot through with silver threads. Meeting Madame Beaudoine's gaze, she whispered, "Did you ask the faeries to add a bit of magic to the gown?"

The modiste's light laughter had Addy smiling in return. "I cannot give away all of my secrets, Madame Fernside."

"I never dreamed to own such a beautiful gown, madame—and on such short notice. Thank you."

"*Mon plaisir.* My pleasure. Monsieur Broadbank has asked me to send a few appropriate gowns, and a riding habit, for you to wear until I can create your new wardrobe for you."

"Oh, but I do not need—"

"*Alors!* Never refuse the offer of a new wardrobe. You will hurt your generous husband's feelings."

"Do not worry about the expense, Addy," Gemma added. "Having been in your place a little over a year ago, I can assure you that the Broadbank men never do anything unless they wish to." She shook her head. "At times it is most trying, though at other times, you will feel as if you are on top of the world. Be patient with Edmund. He is a good man, as is my Colin."

Addy felt warmed by Gemma's words. "Thank you for sharing that with me. I shall take your words to heart."

Madame Beaudoine inclined her head. "Do not forget, it is your duty to be turned out in the latest fashion so you do not shame Monsieur Broadbank or his brother Viscount Moreland. *Oui?*"

"*Oui*...er...yes, madame."

The modiste clapped her hands, and her assistant Yvette returned with two gowns, one a lovely shade of deep blue embellished with a minimum of lace and the other a gown in the deepest of greens. "Monsieur suggested that *ton fils*—your son—may attempt to chew on the lace. Otherwise, I would have added a bit more flourish."

Gemma and Addy shared a smile, then Addy remarked, "Edmund is quite observant. Adam would indeed attempt to either chew on the lace or poke his fingers through the holes."

"I will ensure you do not have too many frills in the everyday gowns I shall create for you." After motioning for Yvette to join her, the madame grasped Addy's hands. "We shall return at the end of the week with fabric samples and my latest designs." Turning to Gemma, she added, "I have a few designs that you will love—they allow room for the little one to grow, while at the same time have everyone commenting on how beautiful and glowing Viscountess Moreland appears."

Tears welled in Gemma's eyes and spilled over.

Addy handed the viscountess her handkerchief. "Don't try to stop the tears. If you are like my sister, your emotions will be up one moment and down the next."

"I shall return at the end of the week," the modiste continued. "Expect to spend a few hours with Yvette and myself. We will poke and prod you, while you try on one gorgeous gown after another."

"I shall have to discuss this with Edmund," Addy said. "I do not need any other gowns. I have a few serviceable ones. Chasing after Adam tends to be quite hard on my clothing."

The madame waved her hand in the air as she walked to the door. "Friday, *mesdames*. Mrs. Fernside, I expect you to be in a more accommodating frame of mind. *Oui?*"

Addy glanced at Gemma, who looked as if she were biting the inside of her cheek to keep from laughing. What else could she do but agree? "*Oui*, madame."

Adam was running up and down the hallway between the back entrance and the kitchen when she stepped into the servants' side of the town house. Horrified that he would interrupt the viscount's staff, she gasped. "Adam, no!"

Startled, he looked over his shoulder, stumbled, and fell on his bottom. His wail could no doubt be heard on the third floor.

"Oh, my love. I am so sorry. I did not mean to scare you." She wiped his tears and gathered him into her arms. His head fell to her shoulder as his sobs lessened. "I was going to ask if you were a good boy while Gemma and I met with the modiste. Remember what I told you? We run outside and we walk inside."

"Forgive me, Addy," Edmund said as he walked into the hallway.

Her gaze shot up, and she knew Adam was not totally at fault. "Edmund, did you encourage Adam to run while Dorothy and her staff were trying to prepare our wedding dinner?"

Instead of answering her question, he furrowed his brow. "Who is Dorothy?"

Addy laughed. "Your cook's name is Dorothy."

"It is? I had no idea. Father always called her Cook. You have been here for a day and you already discovered our cook's name."

"You could have asked her yourself if you were interested."

Edmund did not agree: "Once our father decrees something, it is best not to disagree unless you are ready for a shouting match."

"Ah. Speaking in loud tones must run in the family."

He snorted to cover his laughter. Adam lifted his head and stared at him until Edmund started to laugh. "I supposed they do, Addy. Now, are you ready for a bite of lunch, or would you rather wait until teatime and enjoy a few of Cook's—er...Dorothy's finger sandwiches, followed by cream tarts and teacake?"

"I would love a cup of tea. I'm rather parched after speaking with Madame Beaudoine."

"I take it things went well?"

"They did, though I had hoped Gemma would intervene on my behalf when I tried to dissuade Madame Beaudoine from creating an entire wardrobe for me."

"I promised her a bonus if she created at least a dozen gowns and one riding habit as soon as possible."

Addy gasped. "What on earth will I do with that many gowns?"

HE REACHED FOR her hand. "Wear them to please me." Unable to resist, he pressed a kiss to the end of her upturned nose.

The soft snuffling sound had them both looking at the little one falling asleep against her breast. "I'd best put Adam down for a nap," she said.

"Why don't I have a tray sent to your bedchamber? That way you can relax and mayhap close your eyes for a little while after you have your tea."

"I normally do not rest during the day, but Adam was up before the sun this morning."

Wrapping his arm around her slender waist, he drew her close and brushed a swift kiss to her tempting lips. "Rest, my love. After teatime, there will not be an opportunity for you or Adam to do so until after we are wed."

He wanted to tell her to rest because he intended to join her in their marriage bed, convincing her to trust him with her heart as well as her body. Once they were well and truly one, he would stop worrying that Addy or Adam would be taken from him.

"Shall I accompany you upstairs?" he asked.

"Would you? At Thorne House, I have rooms on the ground floor. I'm not used to carrying Adam up and down staircases yet, but I shall endeavor to become accustomed to doing so."

"Here," he said, reaching for the little boy. "Let me." Pleased when Adam opened his eyes to peer at him before settling down against his chest, Edmund motioned for Addy to precede him. They returned to the main part of the town house and ascended the staircase.

Noting how Addy's steps slowed, he worried what might have happened if he had not been nearby, ready to lend a hand. Striking that useless thought from his head, he reasoned he *was* here and had been able to help.

She opened the door to her bedchamber and let him enter first. "I should change him before you put him down."

"Won't that wake him?"

She shook her head. "He's a very sound sleeper."

Once Adam was in dry nappies and one of his sleeping gowns, they tucked him in.

Warmth speared through him as he stood beside Addy, watching their nephew squirm and scoot until he found a comfortable position to sleep in—with his little backside in the air!

"Are you ever afraid, Addy?" Edmund asked.

"Of what?"

He exhaled heavily. "Everything! Raising a child is a daunting task. I've listened to the lists of things to do and not to do as Colin dictates them to me. He's becoming an expert in order to be there for Gemma and their babe…but so much can go very wrong."

She slipped her arm through his. "But so many things can go right. The most important thing I've learned since Adam was born is to love him. Accept that his fussiness is his frustration as he learns more words to communicate his feelings with us. He's angry when he is too small to figure out how things work...doors opening and closing, how to climb out of his crib, not running inside, but free to run outside."

A feeling of rightness settled over him as they continued to listen to the rhythmic breathing of the child they would raise between them. "I was blessed to find you and Adam when I did. Colin and I agree, our brother would have wanted us to ensure you and Adam had a roof over your heads, food in your bellies, and clothes on your back."

"That could have been accomplished by hiring me on as one of your staff, Edmund. Surely you realize that."

He brushed a wisp of honey-blonde out of her eyes and sighed. "We have a full staff. The only way to be certain our nephew is raised knowing all that he was born to inherit—the responsibilities as well as wealth—is for him to be raised by either Colin or myself."

"Not the earl?"

Edmund's snort of laughter had Adam's eyes popping open and his little face scrunching in a frown.

Before he dissolved into tears, Addy rubbed his back, soothing him back to sleep. "One thing you must remember—loud noises and voices startle little ones. Your brother will soon find that out for himself."

"I shall remember your wise words, Adelaide, and leave you to your rest. There is much to discuss after we are wed." Staring into her siren's eyes, he rasped, "Much to discover."

Her shiver of awareness pleased him.

He lowered his mouth to hers, tasting her lips more fully this time, eager to test his theory that she was as affected by his nearness as he was by hers.

Her soft moan and sweet lips had his head spinning. With the tip of his tongue, he traced the rim of her mouth before deepening the kiss. She tasted of summer sunshine and ripe red berries.

The lingering scent of lavender filled his senses as she wrapped her arms around him, responding to his kiss. One taste would never be enough. Her name on his lips, her scent tantalizing his brain, he slid a hand down her spine to the small of her back, easing her more firmly against him.

His control was slipping by the heartbeat. Bloody hell! He had to step back now.

"We can continue this exploration later," he rasped. "When it is just the two of us." The confusion in her gaze warred with the passion he sensed she had no idea what to do with. "I look forward to tracing the tip of my tongue from beneath your ear to the base of your throat. From the hollow between your collar bones to your breasts and beyond."

Heart pumping, gazes locked, he yanked her to him one last time, plundering her lips. When she sagged against him, he drew one last succulent taste from her sweet mouth to tide him over. "Tonight," he said.

The need to carry her over to the bed, lay her down, and lose himself in her welcoming warmth had him clamping his jaw shut. He inclined his head and left without another word.

God help him, one more kiss...one more tantalizing whiff of her lavender-scented skin and he would lose control!

Drawing in a deep breath and then another, he calmed his racing heart, reminding himself that he needed to go slowly. Woo her with honeyed words, bring her to peak with his lips and tongue before he made love to her.

He needed to blow off steam, or else he would frighten his bride-to-be with his ardor.

Physical exertion would help him regain his ironclad control. Stalking along the hallway, he headed for the servants' staircase and descended. Time to work it off—mayhap Hanson would need a few barrels of supplies moved, or their stable master would need someone to exercise the horses.

Anything to quench the fire raging inside of him.

HAND TO HER throat, Addy stared at the closed door, willing her heartbeat to slow. Her lips still tingled from his kiss. Lord, she never knew one could be swept away and caught up in what she recognized as passion, and she was uneasy with how quickly it had threatened to drag her under.

When he'd drawn her close to him, she could not hear above the pounding of her heart. His firm lips seemed to be demanding she acquiesce to him. She knew what was expected in the marriage bed, but she'd never dreamed to marry. Her life had been spent caring for her younger sister and then her infant nephew.

Edmund's kiss had her wondering if what she'd heard about submitting to her husband's baser needs while imagining herself elsewhere was the truth. She sighed again. It didn't seem possible when the press of his mouth to hers transported her in mind, body, and spirit to a world heretofore unknown to her.

Pressing a hand to her belly, she drew in a deep breath and slowly exhaled. "There is much to be done." The words galvanized her into action. She poured lukewarm water into the blue and white ceramic bowl. Lifting the small round of soap to her nose, she inhaled the faint scent of sun-warmed lavender and relaxed. She worked up a lather and washed her face, neck, and hands, then carefully dried herself. It would not do to dampen the delicate fabric of the dress she would wear to wed the man who'd turned her inside out with his kisses.

The knock on the door had her whirling around. Not wanting her nephew to wake, she opened the door and smiled at Mrs. Pritchard and Gemma. When she put her finger to her lips, the women inclined their heads. The housekeeper motioned for the viscountess to precede her before nodding to the footman carrying the tea tray to set it on the writing desk beneath the window. He bowed and left as quietly as he'd entered.

"Thank you," Addy whispered. "Adam rose so early this morning. I'm hoping he will nap for at least an hour. I wouldn't want him to be fussy later when Edmund and I…"

The words stuck in her throat and her shoulders slumped forward. *Marry*. A simple word that held so much meaning. A promise. A vow. An agreement between a man and a woman to bind themselves to one another for the whole of their lives.

Addy was unsure if she was strong enough to face a life with the handsome man who'd been searching for her—believing she was Adam's mother, when in fact she was his aunt. Would she be able to live up to his expectations? He'd mentioned discoveries. She had the feeling he did not mean unearthing pertinent facts that none but those close to her knew. Concentrating on the inane and not the unknown eased her fear. Would he ask if she took one spoonful or two of sugar in her tea? Mayhap he'd inquire as to her favorite color, or if she knew how to ride or was afraid of horses?

"Would you like me to pour, your ladyship?" the housekeeper asked, interrupting her thoughts.

"No thank you, Mrs. Pritchard. I shall keep Addy company until we've emptied the pot and she is ready to rest."

"Ring if you need anything."

"I will, thank you."

After Mrs. Pritchard left, Gemma asked, "Why don't you sit down while I pour you a cup of tea?"

"Er…yes…thank you. That would be lovely." Gemma nodded toward the rocking chair someone had thoughtfully placed in the bedchamber, but Addy shook her head. "You take the rocking chair. I feel bad that you are here when you should be resting yourself."

"I rest when I'm tired," Gemma assured her. Waiting for Addy to sit in the chair by the desk, she commented, "It is normal that you feel a bit of nerves before your wedding. Is there anything you'd like to ask me?"

Addy smiled. "You are very kind to offer, but I know what to expect in the marriage bed."

"I do hope you will not be shocked when you discover that the pain is fleeting and pleasure will have you gasping for breath while you hold on to the man who will teach you what transpires between a man and his wife behind closed doors."

Intrigued, Addy set her teacup on the desk and scooted her chair closer to Gemma. "Gasping for breath?"

Instead of launching into a retelling of what Addy could expect on her wedding night, Gemma told her to trust her husband not to hurt her when he sought to teach her how the touch of his hand, or the press of his lips, would awaken feelings she could not imagine.

"Feelings?"

The flush on Gemma's face had Addy realizing her question embarrassed her new friend. "It would be best if you asked Edmund. Trust that he wants you to experience pleasure in the marriage act."

"Will he?"

Gemma giggled.

"I take your laughter to indicate he will." Addy paused for a moment as worry filled her. "What if he doesn't? What if I do something wrong? Dear Lord, what if I laugh? I tend to do that when I am nervous."

Gemma set her teacup down and reached for Addy's hand. "Tell him ahead of time that you laugh when you are nervous. Then he will expect it."

"But if I do something wrong?"

"If he is anything like his brother, he will be a patient teacher. Trust me, he will reap the rewards of his patient tutelage."

Addy could only imagine what awaited her. "My knees went weak when he kissed me earlier."

Gemma's eyes gleamed. "Did they? Tell me—No. Wait! Don't tell me. You will think I am wicked to delight in sharing intimate details." She covered her face with her hands and moaned.

Addy could not help but laugh at Gemma's embarrassment. "Forgive me, but your frankness has eased the worst of my worry to the point where I am looking forward to tonight."

Gemma lowered her hands to peek at Addy. "Then you won't think me a wanton woman?"

"No. I don't. I think you are a woman madly in love with your husband. If what goes on behind closed doors adds to that closeness…and results in a babe, how could that be wrong?"

Gemma blinked back tears. "Thank you. I was so scared on our wedding night, but Colin assured me by taking his time and answering any questions I had. I wanted to help ease your nerves and assure you that if you open up and tell Edmund of your fears, he will assuage them."

"I am beyond grateful to you, Gemma. My sister and I…" Addy paused. "The last few years have been difficult. I never expected to be raising her son, but he is now more son than nephew to me. I would not change that for anything in the world."

"Anyone can see the bond between the two of you. Trust Edmund."

"I will. Thank you, Gemma."

"It is my pleasure. I have asked Maisy to watch Adam while you enjoy a nice soak in a hot tub. Then she will help you dress—if that is agreeable to you."

"That sounds lovely. Thank you."

A few moments later, a footman arrived to take the tray. Gemma followed behind him, leaving Addy to wonder at her good fortune. Lying down on the bed, she drew the coverlet up to her chin and closed her eyes. She would marry the handsome man who'd stolen her heart the first time he held Adam in his arms. As she drifted off to sleep, she dreamed she was once more in his arms, delighting in his passionate kisses.

Chapter Nineteen

Edmund stared at the beauty walking toward him on his brother's arm. Strands of honey-colored silk framed her face, leaving him to wonder if her hair reached her shoulders, the middle of her back, or her waist. Would he be able to wrap it around his wrists as he drew her to him…

"…from this day forward?"

The jab to his ribs had him frowning at Colin, who glared at him and mouthed, *Pay attention!* Remembering his line, he cleared his throat and stated in a clear voice, "I do." Out of the side of his eye, he saw his brother's nod of approval.

His thoughts returned to thoughts of her hair, and this time it was a curtain that fell like rain around him as she leaned down and pressed her lips to his…

"What God has joined, let no man pull asunder."

The second jab to his ribs caught him by surprise.

His murmured protest had the vicar frowning at him. "You may kiss your bride."

Edmund's gaze sought Addy's. Emotions swirled in the blue-green depths of her eyes. Nerves mingled with excitement and anticipation.

He dipped his head to brush her mouth with a featherlight kiss. Watching her lids lower, he pulled her closer and nipped at her lips before claiming his bride in an all-consuming kiss, sampling the lush bounty that awaited him.

The voices surrounding them faded as his will faltered and his desire for her threatened to pull him under. The hard grip on his shoulder got his attention—and his ardor back to where it needed to be. At least for the next hour or so.

"Time enough for that after we eat," Colin reminded him.

Addy's face turned a delightful rose, highlighting the curve of her cheek and the tilt of her lips. Her smile warmed his heart.

"Are you hungry, Mrs. Broadbank?" Edmund asked.

"Famished. If you remember, I was too nervous to eat earlier."

Pulling her against him, he leaned down and whispered, "I'd best feed you, since I plan to keep you awake most of the night."

His brother's snort of laughter, coupled with a deep cough, had him realizing the depth of his voice must have carried farther than he'd intended. As he passed his brother, leading his bride into the dining room, he hit Colin with his shoulder.

Colin laughed as he and Gemma followed behind them.

Once everyone was seated, the viscount stood and raised his glass. "A toast, to my brother Edmund! May he and Adelaide's days be filled with happiness and their lives be blessed with children—an even dozen, Lord, if you can manage it."

The laughter that erupted after Colin's toast didn't bother Edmund in the least. He planned to enjoy teaching his bride that there was more to the marriage bed than their joining...the secret places that would unlock the door to the passion he sensed lay dormant, waiting for him to set it free. He could not wait to ignite the flame that, before the night's end, would consume them both.

Addy leaned close to ask, "Is the meal not to your liking? The roast is delicious, as are the potatoes and greens."

He smiled and confessed, "My thoughts keep straying to—" The sound of his brother loudly clearing his throat made Edmund realize it was best to remain in the here and now. "Forgive me, Addy. My thoughts were elsewhere."

His wife's hands were trembling as she reached for her wineglass to sip from it. Needing to soothe her worry, he pressed his thigh against hers. Her gasp had him groaning inwardly as he reached for the glass that slipped from her fingers. Setting it down, he rose from his seat and held out his hand to his wife.

"Thank you all for coming tonight to witness our vows," he announced to the room. "Please stay and enjoy your meal."

To the delight of those gathered, he swept Addy into his arms and strode from the room. The rumble of his brother's voice offering a second toast had him quickening his pace.

"Edmund!" Addy squealed. "Put me down."

He laughed and jogged toward the staircase. "Not until we are behind closed...*locked* doors."

"But Edm—"

He cut off her protests with his mouth. "I do not want to have to speak to anyone again until tomorrow—or the next day."

"What about Adam?" she protested. "He is just a little boy."

"Who loves his auntie Gemma, Maisy...and my blowhard of a brother."

Her answering giggle had him beaming as he shifted her in his arms. He opened the door to his bedchamber and kicked it closed before setting her on her feet.

"Thank God, we're finally alone!" He locked the door and pulled her into his embrace. "Have I told you how beautiful you are, Mrs. Broadbank?"

"I uh...don't remember." Struggling to ease a step back from him, she said, "Edmund, I thought you wanted to discuss our marriage."

His gaze never left hers. "I do...later."

"But how will we know what we are going to say when people ask how we met, or why there was no announcement, or engagement?"

He laughed. "We tell them it's none of their bloody business."

Her eyebrows lifted. "I thought I would have a little more time before we sealed our vows. Wasn't it to be more a marriage of convenience and Adam's protection and that of your family's name and the viscountcy?"

"I didn't think you would marry me if I told you how I felt the first time we met." He slowly drew her closer. "Your siren's eyes beckoned to me, while your lips trembled whenever I dared to let my gaze touch them."

SHE SIGHED AND stopped resisting. "I thought you agreed to the marriage because you signed an agreement with Mrs. Dove-Lyon."

"I could have easily doubled her fee. She would have set fire to it without blinking."

Gemma's earlier conversation filled her mind as she stared at the strong line of his jaw, daring to reach up and brush the tips of her fingers on the shadow of the beard that had darkened as the day wore on.

His gaze softened. "Have you never touched a man's face before?"

She shook her head.

"If I am attending an evening function, I normally must shave again. My brothers and I were all cursed with a heavy, dark beard." When she let her hand slip away, he held it to his face and sighed. "Please," he rasped. "Touch me."

Wanting to feel the press of his lips, she stood on her toes and boldly kissed him. Edmund wrapped his arms around her as he groaned and plundered. He teased her lips apart and dipped the tip of his tongue between them for a fuller tasting.

She could not contain her gasp of surprise or moan of pleasure. He responded by sweeping his tongue into her mouth, dueling with hers. The masterful way he probed with his tongue, then retreated to trace a line of kisses along the underside of her jaw, had her legs simply giving out.

He swept her into his arms again and walked over to the bed. Going down on one knee, he placed her in the middle, drew back, and stared at her. "God, you are so beautiful. I ache to make you mine, Addy."

She giggled and covered her mouth with both hands.

His answering frown had her remembering Gemma's advice and slowly lowering her hands. "I'm so sorry. I meant to tell you."

His look darkened as he straightened and took a step back. "Tell me what?"

"When I am very nervous, I laugh."

His intense look changed to one of speculation. "Do you?" As if to test her theory, he leaned over the bed until their lips were a breath apart. "Am I making you nervous?"

She shook her head, but another soft giggle burst from between her lips. A tear slipped past her guard. "I'm sorry, Edmund, but I don't know what to do. I mean, I do, but I've never…"

Unable to meet his gaze, she closed her eyes and gave in to the tears.

"Addy, my love. Don't cry." She felt the bed dip under his weight as he cuddled her against his broad chest. His heat lulled her, while his words soothed her. "You have no reason to fear me. I will not force you, but for Adam's sake, we must consummate our marriage to be well and truly wed in the eyes of the law and the church."

"I understand."

He brushed a kiss to her brow. "Why don't I help you undress, then you can help me?"

She could not help but be shocked. Obviously there was more to this consummating than she'd previously considered. "Undress you?"

"I wouldn't want either of us to get caught in a tangle of cotton, satin, and the ethereal blue-green overlay that matches your eyes."

"But I thought we would change," she began, only to bite her lip.

"Change what? My mind? My darling, I will not change my mind."

Yet another giggle escaped before she could cover her mouth. "Forgive me."

His answer was to cover her mouth with his, drawing the very heart from her breast with each successive kiss. Her limbs felt weak, and her belly felt as if a thousand butterflies fluttered inside of it.

"Tell me what you thought we would change."

"Our clothes." When he didn't contradict her, she asked, "Shall I change into my nightrail now?"

He nipped the end of her nose with his teeth, and she gasped. "Mayhap later. First, I think I shall help you undress so we can discover how your body will react to the brush of my fingertips."

Emboldened by his words, she rasped, "Where?"

"Oh, my darling," he groaned. "Everywhere." Edmund rose from the bed and eased her to her feet. "Turn around, love." He undid her buttons and pressed his lips to the nape of her neck.

She shivered in response.

"Lift your arms, Addy."

She did as he bade and was rewarded with his sharply indrawn breath as she stood before him in her thin batiste chemise.

Entranced, he lifted his gaze to meet hers. "Shall we test my theory?"

"Theory?"

"Mmm...how does it feel when I brush my fingertips from your shoulder to the base of your throat?"

Her belly clenched as an uncontrollable shiver took hold.

"So sweet," he murmured, pressing a line of kisses where his fingertips had been.

Lost in sensation after sensation, she did not realize he had slipped her chemise off one shoulder, baring her breast, until he drew her nipple into the heat of his mouth and suckled her—teasing, tasting, until she was pressing her body against his, begging him to make the ache building inside of her go away.

"Not yet, love," he said. After easing her chemise off her other shoulder, he began the same delicious torture, drawing her other breast into his mouth, suckling, sampling, driving her mad with desire until she demanded he put a stop to it.

His knowing smile and promise to do as she asked relaxed her until she was standing before him with nothing to shield her nakedness from him. Embarrassed to the core, she tried to hide from him. He soothed her with honeyed words as he coaxed her to lie on the bed.

As he removed his frockcoat and waistcoat, she marveled that the width of his shoulders remained unchanged. Her husband did not need buckram padding added to fill out his frockcoat. When he removed his cravat and cambric shirt, her breath caught in her lungs. The beautifully sculpted muscles of his chest and abdomen begged to be touched. She reached out a hand to do just that, but drew it back when he chuckled.

"Are you nervous?"

EDMUND DID NOT want to admit that he was amused by her reaction to his body. He shrugged and let her believe he had a similar habit of laughing when he was nervous.

"You are beautiful, Edmund—are those stitches in your arm?"

"Aye. I was going to ask Cook to remove them tomorrow."

"I'm sorry that I'd forgotten about your injuries and my promise to care of them for you."

"We had other things to worry about, my love. The wound is healing—there is nothing to be concerned about."

"You are certain?"

The worry in her gaze warmed his heart. He inclined his head and undid the placket on his trousers. Unsure of her reaction, he quickly removed them, completely undone by the way she stared at him. Not wanting to hide anything from her, he drew in a breath and let his body react to her inquisitive gaze.

When her mouth hung open, he knew he was more than ready to make love to his wife—though *she* was not quite ready.

Joining her on the bed, he drew her into his arms and shifted until she lay beneath him. He nudged her legs apart and settled between them.

Her heat seared him as she lifted her gaze to his. "It's going to hurt, isn't it?"

"Only this once."

"You should probably get it over with." His sharp bark of laughter had her frowning at him. "That was not meant to be funny."

"I know, but if you could see the determination on your face…" He paused, then asked, "Do you remember my other theory?"

"Which one?"

"About brushing the tips of my fingers all over you?"

She swallowed audibly. "Yes."

"Let's give that a try." He rolled onto his side and brushed his fingertips over her breasts again and again until she was writhing in his arms. He trailed them lower, slowly inching closer to her belly until he brushed against the very heat of her. When she softly moaned, he ran his fingers along the inside of her thighs.

She quivered with need. "Edmund."

"Aye, love?"

"I ache."

"I know."

"Make it stop."

"Not quite yet." He leaned close and captured her lips in a drugging kiss as his fingers circled her heat before slipping inside of her. He groaned at the slickness begging him for more.

Her gasp was swallowed by another deep kiss, as his cock replaced his fingers, probing deeper. When he met the resistance of her maidenhead, he lifted his gaze to meet hers. Her eyes were glazed with a mixture of shock and desire.

"The pain will ease, I promise you. Trust me."

"I do."

He lifted his hips and filled her to the hilt. When they were fully joined, he waited for her to relax, so the pain would ease. He wished he could make it recede faster. "I'm so sorry, Addy, but it truly is only for the first time."

"It's almost gone. Are you finished?" His deep, rumbling laughter had her smiling. "Are you nervous again, or relieved it's over?"

"My love, it has only just begun."

He began a rhythm as old as time itself, plunging, withdrawing, and then thrusting again. She lifted her hips, meeting him as they drove one another closer to the edge of oblivion. She gasped his name, and he thrust one last time, pouring his seed into her.

Rolling so she was on top of him, he drew the coverlet up to her shoulders and slipped his hand down to the curve of her backside and along the length of her spine. Again and again, until he felt her heartbeat slow and her breathing change.

Certain she slept, he whispered the words he was not certain she was ready to hear—"I love you, Addy"—as exhaustion dragged him under.

Chapter Twenty

"Are you ready to rejoin the family, love?"

Addy did not want to let go of her husband. Resting her head against his chest, she marveled at the way his voice rumbled beneath her ear. "Five minutes more?"

His chuckle added another layer to the vibration beneath her ear. "If we wait much longer, my brother will pound on the door until we open it. Patience is not one of Colin's virtues."

She could not contain her laughter. "Nor is his ability to control the volume of his voice."

"That will not be our problem much longer," Edmund reminded her. "Shall we join the family for breakfast?"

She sighed. "Do you think anyone will put up a fuss when we tell them of our plans to live at Thorne House?"

Releasing her, he pressed a kiss to her forehead, then placed a hand to her waist as he opened the door for her. "My brother and Gemma offered Templeton House as our home. There is plenty of room, but I am quite certain they will understand our desire to begin our married life in our own home. Although Gemma may ask you to stay for a prolonged visit before and after their babe is born."

"I would love to come back for a visit but hate to let Grandmother's estate fall further into ruin with only a handful of pensioners in residence. Mr. and Mrs. Wythe are a lovely older couple, but they work too hard."

"Ah yes," he said as they descended the stairs. "Brother to Miss Wythe, with whom you were staying while in London."

"She seems a bit lonely. I wonder if she would agree to come and live at Thorne House?"

"We may not have time to stop and see her when we leave. Why not write to her?"

Addy paused outside of the dining room. "You would not mind?"

"Not in the least. Anything that will make you happy."

She placed her hand on his forearm, unsure of herself. "I would not want you to think I am trying to control your life. You're already giving up so much by acquiescing to my request that we return to Thorne House."

He paused in front of the closed doors. "I am looking forward to getting involved with the running of your grandmother's estate. From what you've said, it has been some time since there was an excess of coin, time, or attention poured into it. I would love nothing more than getting my hands dirty."

She studied him before saying, "You really mean that, don't you?"

IRRITATION BUBBLED TOO close to the surface for his liking. He thrust it back. "Do you doubt my word?"

"No!"

Her emphatic reply made him study her closely for a few moments before inclining his head.

"It is just that you are a gentleman," she said, "and I've never met one who was willing to work planting or plowing."

He grinned. "I prefer thatching and digging and have been known to whistle while mucking out a horse stall."

She hugged him close and whispered, "You are almost too good to be real. I keep wondering if I am dreaming."

He bent his head and captured her lips. "What we have shared for the last two days has been the stuff of dreams, Addy my love. It is time to return to our duties, though I promise to continue our nightly routine of putting Adam to bed together before retiring to continue experimenting with my theories."

"You have the most wonderful theories, Edmund. I should love to continue exploring new places with you."

He groaned with need. The urge to toss her over his shoulder and return to his bedchamber consumed him, but reason intruded. They needed to return to their duties. Addy's to care for little Adam, his to speak privately to his brother to receive the latest updates as to whether Honeywell had been brought in for questioning.

"Edmund, do you promise now that we are wed, we will not go our separate ways?"

Actions spoke louder than words. He hauled her against him and savored the warmth of her embrace, the sweetness of her kiss.

"Ahem!"

He lifted his lips enough to mumble, "Go away, Colin."

"Someone wants to see his mother and father," his brother said.

Addy slipped from his arms and beamed at Adam. "Oh, I've missed you," she declared.

Edmund silently wondered when she would have had the time. They'd spent most of the last forty-eight hours wrapped in one another's arms. He could not wait to make love to his wife again—mayhap after lunch, before teatime.

"No," his brother growled.

"No what?" Edmund asked, though he suspected his brother had read his mind.

"We have two meetings back to back directly after breakfast. Then it's on to—"

"We shall be packing," Edmund interrupted.

"Where in the bloody hell are you going?"

ADDY TURNED WITH Adam in her arms. "We planned to discuss it with you over breakfast." When neither Edmund nor Colin spoke, she turned her back on them and, nodding to the footmen on either side of the doors, said, "Good morning."

They greeted her and swept open the doors.

"There you are." Gemma smiled as she studied Addy from head to toe. "You are looking…rested."

Addy flushed as she settled into the chair next to her sister-in-law. Leaning close, she whispered, "You were right."

Delighted, Gemma asked, "About what?"

Addy laughed. "All of it!"

They were chatting and giggling when the men entered the dining room. "Good morning, Gemma," Edmund said.

"Good morning, Edmund. You are looking…rested."

His sharp bark of laughter in response seemed to please Gemma immensely. "So wonderful to see the two of you getting along."

"*Gemma.*" Colin's tone held a note of warning that his wife gleefully ignored.

"Now then, what are your plans for the day?" Gemma asked.

"They're packing," the viscount informed her.

Hand to her breast, Gemma turned to Addy. "But you just got

here!"

Addy grasped her sister-in-law's hand. "Edmund and I think it's best, given the circumstances—and what he has yet to divulge about what happened the night before we wed..." Frowning at her husband, she continued, "Something involving the Dark Walk—"

"Colin," Edmund interrupted. "What time are Coventry and King arriving?"

"Three-quarters of an hour from now," Colin responded.

"So early?" Gemma inquired.

The viscount ignored his wife. "Do you need to take the state coach to Thorne House, or would you prefer one of our smaller carriages?"

"Small would be better," Edmund replied. "No family crest on the side."

"Are we traveling incognito?" Addy asked.

Both men ignored her question, too. Colin turned to his brother. "Would you care to choose the horses for your journey?"

Gemma pushed back her chair and stood. "Come, Addy—I shall help you pack."

Colin and Edmund stood between their wives and the door.

"Gemma, you haven't eaten," Colin said.

She lifted her chin and glared at her husband. "I seem to have lost my appetite." She slipped past him and stood in the doorway.

Addy stepped around Colin and linked her arm with Gemma's. "As have I. We shall leave you to your private discussions."

With a swirl of skirts—and irritation—the women swept from the room.

"WE SHALL NEVER hear the end of it," Colin warned his brother.

"Tell me what's happened."

"Not here," the viscount said. He told the nearest footman, "Please ask Cook to send breakfast to our wives in Gemma's bedchamber."

"At once, your lordship."

When Edmund took a step toward the door, his brother called him back. "Let them stew for a bit—it won't hurt them, and we need to eat. We cannot come up with a solid plan on an empty stomach."

They ate in companionable silence. When they'd finished, Colin cleared his throat and said, "You look...*rested*."

Edmund snorted, and tea shot out his nose. "Bloody hell, that hurts!"

Colin roared with laughter and handed his napkin to his brother. "I wasn't asking if you rested, just making a comment that whatever you were doing for the last forty-eight hours...you look—"

"Rested," Edmund growled. "You're such a pain in the *arse*."

They were laughing when Hanson entered the dining room to announce, "Captain Coventry and Gavin King have arrived."

The men rose from the table. "Excellent," Colin said.

"I've shown them to the library as you requested, your lordship."

"Thank you, Hanson."

Coventry and King were in deep discussion when the brothers walked into the library. "Gentlemen," the viscount said. "Thank you for coming so quickly."

Edmund didn't bother with greetings. "Has Honeywell been detained?"

"Last night," King replied.

"He was released early this morning," Coventry added.

King scrubbed a hand over his face. "Blackmailing a peer is an offense, though not as serious as other offenses."

"And in light of the fact that the men in custody cannot be directly connected to Honeywell..."

"What about Redfern's statement?" Edmund rasped. "Have they dismissed his claims?"

Coventry shook his head. "They are being investigated. We should hear by this afternoon. By the by, thank you for giving me Redfern's direction. He agreed to come on board after he sees my physician."

Concerned, Edmund asked, "Is he ill?"

"I asked if he had been fitted for a prosthesis. Apparently he had but did not have the coin to cover the cost. Homemade crutches were all he could afford."

"I shall cover the cost," Edmund offered.

"It has been taken care of," Colin said. "Now then, has anyone questioned Miss Lily Lovecote?"

"Twice," King replied. "She is quite charmingly evasive, though not as guileless as she would like us to believe."

"The opposite of her sister," Edmund said.

"I was surprised to hear our information was not accurate," King admitted, "but relieved to discover that it was accurate as to who paid a visit to Templeton House last year."

"Aye," Coventry agreed. "Just not in the assumption that the woman was indeed the actress purported to have had an affair with your brother."

"Adam would never have turned her away," Colin told the men.

"Understood," King replied. "However, the earl—"

"Was grieving," Edmund said in his father's defense. "It has all worked out for the best. Addy, little Adam, and I will be leaving in the morning for Thorne House."

"How many guards will be accompanying you?" King asked.

"We don't need—"

Colin interrupted, "Four."

"No one will bother following us now that Honeywell's blackmail plot has been foiled," Edmund said. "I do not require any guards."

"I see. I thought you would value Addy and Adam's lives. I must have misunderstood."

"Bloody hell, Colin! You know that I do. I think you are overreacting."

"Better to overreact than to find yourself in the middle of the countryside with only pensioners to defend your wife and adopted son."

"As to that," Coventry interjected, "have the papers been signed?"

"We are to meet with the solicitor this afternoon," Edmund replied.

"Adelaide has a letter from her sister asking her to take care of Adam," Colin added.

"Care for Adam," King repeated. "But no mention of giving Adelaide custody of the boy? Even though the lad's father is deceased, this lack of clarity could be contested later."

Coventry asked, "Have either of you informed your father of Edmund's marriage or that you've found Adam's rightful heir?"

Edmund shrugged, and the viscount responded, "Not as yet—we shall tell him in due time."

"I do not envy you that particular discussion," King remarked. "If you are sending four of your men with Edmund and his family, would you like me to send a few men to you on temporary assignment?"

"Not necessary, but thank you for the offer."

"I wasn't aware that you had that many retired seamen working for you," Edmund said.

Coventry grinned. "Between Colin and I, we have men who will be taking over guard duty here."

"I hate to keep pressing a point," King said, "but until this matter has been fully resolved—and it won't be until the adoption papers have been finalized, and the connection to Honeywell has been firmly verified—we cannot be too careful."

"Power corrupts," the viscount stated.

Edmund nodded. "Greed is a powerful enemy."

"Be on your guard at all times, Broadbank," King warned.

"My brother knows to watch his back," Colin said.

"And between us," Coventry added, "our men will see to it that your family is well protected."

"Thank you," Edmund replied. "I was a bit worried when Addy mentioned the age of Mr. Wythe and his wife—they are in their late seventies."

"Are you certain four men is enough?" King asked. "Are there any tenant farms on the property?"

"A few, though I don't believe Addy mentioned how many. The estate was bequeathed to her by her grandmother." A thought occurred to Edmund as he mentioned it. "Addy is the older sister—should anything happen to her…"

"Good God!" Colin said. "If Honeywell knows this, your wife could be next in his sights."

Fear ripped through Edmund, shredding his confidence. "I never thought I'd be doing this, but for my wife and little Adam's sake, King, I believe I'll take you up on your offer of more men."

"Consider it done," the older man replied. "I shall hand-pick six men to accompany you to Thorne House. Can you delay leaving until midday tomorrow?"

"Aye."

"My men and I should be here before noon at the earliest, two o'clock at the latest."

Edmund offered his hand. "Thank you, King."

"My pleasure, Broadbank." Turning to the viscount, King again offered his hand.

Colin shook it. "I shall keep in close contact with yourself and Coventry. My brother will too."

"I can speak for myself," Edmund shot back.

"Aye, but you did not. One of us had to state your intentions."

Coventry chuckled as he bade the brothers goodbye and left in King's wake.

Once the pair were in the hallway, King turned to Coventry and said, "We need to send a detail of men to Moreland Chase. See if you can convince his lordship to speak to his father. The earl needs to be apprised of the situation."

"Why didn't you mention it before we left?"

King chuckled. "The viscount will have enough to concern himself with, sending men to accompany Broadbank and his family to Leeds. Between us, we shall see to their protection."

Coventry agreed. "On all fronts."

CHAPTER TWENTY-ONE

LILY LOVECOTE OPENED the door to her dressing room and glared at the man standing there. "Really, Honeywell, must you persist in your pursuit even after I have given you your *congé*?"

"Darling, you and I both know that you enjoy the merry chase as much as I do."

He inserted his foot in the door before she could close it, forcing his way into the room.

Irritation was coupled with a hint of unease, but Lily was a consummate actress and becoming quite well known for her talents on…and off the stage. "Do not be tiresome. I only have an hour to prepare before I go on stage. Please take yourself off."

"I will not be swept aside as if I were something distasteful," he warned.

Why had she never noticed the menacing look in his eyes when he was angry? "Leave now, before I shout for the stage manager. I cannot believe you managed to get past him when I expressly told him I was not to be disturbed."

His laugh grated on her nerves. "Everyone knows you are besotted with me, Lily."

Her patience snapped. She knew how to get immediate attention. Tilting her head back, she screamed as if her throat was about to be slashed.

Footsteps pounded toward her dressing room. Before Honeywell could close his mouth, he was dragged from her doorway by a pair of behemoths who dwarfed him.

"Miss Lily, are you hurt?"

"Did he accost you?"

Hand to her throat, she could only shake her head. The man who had been her most recent admirer, one she had considered having an affair with, had shown his true colors a fortnight ago. She had been avoiding him since.

"Don't worry, Miss Lily—he won't bother you again."

"Thank you."

"I wonder how accommodating your sister Adelaide will be when I call on her later tonight," Honeywell sneered.

"Stay away from Addy!" Her breath snagged in her breast... *Adam!*

Dear Lord, did Honeywell know that her son was in her sister's care?

Chapter Twenty-Two

"I CANNOT BELIEVE he's finally tired himself out." Addy stared down at the little boy snuggled in her arms. "I had hoped he would do better on the return carriage ride than he did traveling to London."

"You knew he would be difficult to handle when forced into the confines of a closed carriage," Edmund replied.

She did not want to admit the truth, but her husband's raised brow and tight jaw were all the impetus she needed to confess, "He's so curious and wants to know how everything works."

"The lad cannot sit still for more than five minutes at a time," he grumbled.

"Well, yes," she agreed, "there is that."

"And you did not feel it necessary to share that salient point with me before a journey of this length?"

"In all honesty, Edmund, I was afraid you would not take us home."

"Adelaide."

The rumbling tone of his voice should have been soothing, but there was a tinge of annoyance beneath the surface. She quickly apologized. "Forgive me. Adam misses home as much as I do."

He surprised her by brushing a lock of hair from her eyes and smoothing the tip of his finger along the curve of her cheek. Desire simmering beneath the surface awakened with a jolt that surprised her. New to the passion between them, she reveled at the depth of his desire swirling in his wintry gray gaze.

"There is nothing to forgive, my love. However, if I had known ahead of time, I could have adjusted our plans and made arrangements at another inn or two along the way. It's far easier when they are expecting us to arrive. Extending the trip by another day might also have helped."

Marveling that he seemed able to bank his passion until it smoldered, she knew she would have to attempt to control her need. She drew in a deep breath and exhaled to regain her balance, then said, "By the time we arrive at Thorne House, you will have experienced all of Adam's moods. Delightful, hungry, fractious, hungry, exhausted."

Edmund grinned, adding, "Hungry?"

She leaned against him and sighed. "Although you may not agree, I promise you this trip has been far easier than the last one." His incredulous expression had her reinforcing her words. "Truly. He has been far more manageable having you with us. He quite taken with you, and a bit in awe of you as well."

"As I have not traveled with a small child before, I shall have to acquiesce until I have experienced all of our son's moods."

Addy studied the face of the man that had captivated her from the first. "If anyone prophesized a year ago that I would be responsible for raising my nephew and seeking Mrs. Dove-Lyon's assistance in finding a husband, I would have thought them a candidate for Bedlam!"

"If anyone had told me that I would marry my nephew's aunt, I would have thought the same."

Silence settled between them as Adam slept and their carriage traversed the distance toward the next changes of horse. Her husband seemed deep in thought. After the chaotic last few hours, she felt he deserved a bit of quiet time.

Just when she thought her husband preferred to be alone with his thoughts, he remarked, "Now that I know what to expect, I believe I am more than ready to meet the challenges ahead traveling with our son will bring."

"What will happen to Adam and me if you decide by journey's end that you have had your fill of his rambunctiousness?"

He placed his knuckle beneath her chin, tilting it so their lips were perfectly aligned. "I would have no choice but to kiss you senseless and remind you that I did not say my vows lightly. You, my love, are stuck with me."

BY THE TIME they reached Thorne House the next day, Edmund was more than ready for the journey to be over. He would never admit it to his lovely wife, but it would be some time before he willingly traveled that far a distance with their delightfully active son. At least until he'd found a few more ways to distract the lad so that Adam would cease climbing on the top edge of the squabs and kicking his feet on the carriage door.

Needing the distraction, Edmund turned and stared at the woman seated beside him, at their son quietly resting in her arms. "How is it that you look just as lovely today as you did when I handed you into our carriage?"

Addy beamed at him. "I am used to Adam's moods and his need to explore, and am happy to be home—our home. I'm looking forward to introducing you to Mrs. and Mrs. Wythe. I know you will take to them at once. They will be so pleased to meet you."

"It will be a pleasure to meet them as well—and pay them their back wages."

"They will not be expecting it and will no doubt question you thoroughly before accepting it." She placed her hand on his forearm. "Please do not be vexed with them—they have been taking care of myself and my sister for so long that they are accustomed to economizing."

"I am not an ogre."

"Of course not," she said. "I did not want you to be taken by surprise or be offended that your offers of immediate repayment were repudiated because of their pride—it is what they are used to."

Her words soothed the agitation bubbling to the surface. He would need to remain calm and find his footing at Thorne House. Her grandmother's legacy would be their home, and he would make certain he did all in his power to restore it to its former glory.

"I will need their advice regarding candidates to add to our staff. Given their advanced ages, I do not want to overwork them."

"You are too good, Edmund." She pressed a kiss to his cheek. "Be careful not to mention their age when speaking to them."

He laughed as the coach slowed to a halt in front of Thorne House. "I promise, my dear. Any other words of wisdom?"

She wrinkled her nose at him in reply. Though what in God's name that meant, he had no idea. The smile that followed assured him she was not upset with him. *Excellent.* They would need to present a united front when speaking to the Wythes and in helping Adam adjust to Edmund as his father.

CHAPTER TWENTY-THREE

EDMUND SMILED AT the picture his wife and their nephew made walking toward where he stood at the door to the stables. "And what might you two be up to on this fine day?"

"It is a lovely day, isn't it?" Addy responded, lifting her face to the bright sun. "I missed being in the country. The air is so fresh and the land…beautiful."

"Yes," he agreed, holding her gaze. "Beautiful."

Addy's lilting laughter wrapped around him. "Flatterer."

"You wound me, my love. My words are not meant to flatter you." He lifted her hand to his lips and brushed a kiss to the back of it. "I speak the truth."

She flushed a lovely rose and nodded.

Pleased with her reaction, Edmund bent down and asked Adam, "Would you like to see the horses?"

"Horsies!"

He chuckled as he picked Adam up and offered his arm to Addy.

The warmth of her smile as she accepted it filled him with a sense of rightness. They had settled into Thorne House without a hitch. Additional staff had been hired—to the delight of the Wythes—and repairs to the outbuildings and stables completed.

The press of Addy's body as they walked through the stables filled him with a sense of completeness, rightness. He had not realized he was lonely until the void had been filled by Addy and Adam. He could not imagine his life without them.

In the fortnight they had been living at Thorne House, Edmund had seen a different side of his wife. She was comfortable in the role of mistress of the estate, handling the staff with respect, patience, and concern…given their advanced ages.

They had been welcomed and treated as if they were royalty. Edmund's concern that the Wythes would not be amenable to the new staff he hired from the village had been brushed aside. The older couple had taken the new footmen and maids under their wing, making room for them while assuming their former roles as butler and housekeeper and assigning duties.

"How are Mr. and Mrs. Wythe this afternoon?" Edmund asked.

"Enjoying having returned to their roles," Addy replied. "I had not realized how much they worried about the lack of staff."

"Mayhap it was not the lack of staff so much as it was the amount of work they told me you had taken on yourself."

"I did not have the coin to hire anyone, and I certainly could not ask them to do jobs that I know would be too difficult for them physically, could I?"

"You have a kind heart, my love."

Adam patted his cheek and reminded him, "Horsies!"

He chuckled, leading the way to the first stall. "Gently now," he warned.

Adam bubbled with laughter as he carefully touched the gelding on its velvety muzzle. "Soft."

"That's right, Adam," Addy said. "Very soft."

"Mr. Broadbank?"

Edmund turned and nodded to the footman. "What is it, Giles?"

"A messenger just arrived. Said it was urgent that he speak with you."

Addy put her hand on his arm. "Let me take Adam. We'll stay a bit longer. I'm hoping he'll tire enough to nap."

"You will promise to stay right here?" Edmund asked.

His insistence that he knew her whereabouts at all times was tiring. Though it had been weeks since the incident at the Dark Walk, he had not relented. She sighed before responding, "Yes."

"I shall return directly."

Watching him walk away, she wondered when he would cease to worry. She did not believe they were in constant danger, as Edmund insisted. The close watch he kept on her, and Adam, unnerved her to the point where she felt stifled.

She shook her head. Mayhap her worries were over, because for the first time since they'd arrived, she and Adam were alone in the stables. Addy planned to take advantage of the freedom.

"Now then, my love, would you like to say hello to the other horses?"

Adam babbled with excitement, but he wasn't looking at the horses—he was looking over her shoulder toward the open door.

"Addy!"

She spun around, shock shooting through her. "Lily! What are you doing here? Aren't you supposed to be on the stage?"

Her sister rushed forward, worry in her eyes. "This is all my fault," she said. "You've got to listen carefully. He's coming. I tried to distract him and throw him off my trail, but he knows you and Adam are here."

"Who knows? Lily, are you in trouble?"

Lily didn't answer. She glanced over her shoulder. "Quickly! We must hide Adam!"

Addy picked up on her sister's worry and led her to the tack room on the other side of the large building. After scanning the room to ensure all of the tools were safely stored away out of Adam's reach, she turned back to her sister. "He'll be safe in here." She arranged a few crates to make a hiding spot for him. Kneeling, she brushed her hand over his cheek. "Remember how we played hide-and-seek yesterday?"

He grinned at her, and her heart melted. Though she hated to leave him on his own, she knew it was urgent that she do so.

"You hide here. I will have Edmund come and find you." She held a finger to her lips. "Quiet as a mouse."

"Mouse," Adam agreed in a whisper.

"Will he be quiet?" Lily rasped.

Addy grabbed her sister's hand and looked over her shoulder one more time. Adam was leaning against one of the crates with his thumb in his mouth and his eyes half-closed. "He'll fall asleep."

They reached the side door in time to hear a gruff voice shout, "Lily!"

The sisters froze.

"He's here," Lily whispered. "I have to answer him."

"We should wait for Edmund to return."

"He may have arranged a distraction to draw your husband away from the stables. We cannot afford to wait."

"Who is here?" When her sister ignored the question, fear slithered inside Addy. It nauseated her, but she had no time for hysterics or fear. She had to protect Adam and her sister. "I'll come with you."

Neither noticed the man standing quietly in the doorway, watching them. "Well now, this is a surprise. Lily and her sister...together."

"Lord Honeywell." Lily noted the pistol in his hand. "I'll come with you willingly."

"That's not what you said the last time we spoke. You remember what you said to me that night in your dressing room, don't you, Lily? You told me to take myself off after you refused my offer of protection."

Addy's heart began to pound as she recognized the name. "You're the one who tried to blackmail my brother-in-law!"

He turned toward her. "Clever chit, aren't you?" He motioned with the pistol for her to move closer to Lily. "You are both coming with me."

Addy lifted her chin. She would show the man she was not afraid. "I rather think I *am* clever. Neither one of us is going anywhere with you."

Honeywell turned and aimed his pistol at Addy. "If that is your choice, so be it." He fired.

Addy's shock turned to horror as Lily rammed into her. Her sister's body jerked as Lily took the lead ball meant for her. Addy screamed her sister's name as she fell to her knees.

Angry curses and the sound of fists connecting with flesh behind her did not distract her from saving her sister. She ripped at her skirt, wadded the material, and pressed it against the bloody hole in her sister's chest.

Lily's eyes met hers. "Papers you sent me..." she rasped. "In my reticule."

"Don't try to talk," Addy said, struggling to remain calm.

"Signed them. You are Adam's mum now."

Tears blurred Addy's vision. "I promise to take good care of Adam until you are well."

Her sister gasped for air and whispered, "I'll be his angel." A heartbeat later, she went still in Addy's arms.

Addy stared at her sister, disbelieving how quickly she'd been taken from her. She brushed the tips of her fingers over Lily's lifeless eyes, closing them. Though she knew her sister was gone, a part of her simply could not process that fact. "Please, don't leave us, Lily."

Edmund grunted as he tackled Honeywell from behind, disarming him. Four men raced into the stables, two subduing Honeywell. Edmund then rushed over to Addy's side and dropped to his knees beside his wife and sister-in-law.

"She pushed me out of the way," Addy sobbed, keeping the pressure on her sister's wound.

Edmund took hold of her hands. "Here, let me." He didn't state the obvious—that Lily was no longer breathing. "Where's Adam? I can hear him crying."

"But my sister…"

He gently moved her hands out of the way and placed his where hers had been. "I'll take care of her. One of King's men left to summon the physician as soon as we heard the shot. Go and get our son."

Addy wiped her bloodied hands on her skirts and dashed off toward the tack room. "Don't cry, Adam! Mum's coming."

The child stopped screaming, but she could still hear him crying. She continued talking to him as she unlocked the door. The brave little boy stood in the middle of his hiding spot, tears streaming down his face, bottom lip trembling. "Mum," he wailed. "Want Poppa."

Using her sleeve, she wiped his face and lifted him into her arms, holding him to her heart. "He'll be here soon. Why don't I take you to have milky tea and cakes with Mrs. Wythe?"

"Cake?"

"Yes, my sweet boy. Come." She stepped out of the tack room, careful to turn and shield Adam from the carnage. Edmund rose to his feet and wiped his hands on his frockcoat, then lifted his head and met her gaze. The acute sorrow in his eyes told her what she already knew.

Lily was dead.

CHAPTER TWENTY-FOUR

THE REST OF the afternoon passed in a blur, except for a few moments that Addy distinctly remembered—Maisy's eyes filled as she saw the blood on Addy's gown, but one stern look from Addy, and the maid blinked back her tears and took Adam from her to find Mrs. Wythe and the promised treat.

The other moment Addy relived over and over again was her sister slamming into her and jerking as the lead ball lodged deep in Lily's chest. Addy stared at her hands for the hundredth time, wondering if someone had washed the blood away. She didn't remember doing so.

"Addy, love?"

The familiar voice had her lifting her head. "Edmund."

"Adam's with Maisy. She'll tuck him in for his afternoon nap."

Why were her arms and legs so heavy? She couldn't seem to gather the strength to stand.

"I need you to be strong and hold on for just a little while longer." He took hold of her hands and pulled her to her feet. "Can you do that for me, love?"

"Yes." She did not want to, but he'd asked so nicely, how could she refuse? "What do you need me to do?"

"Captain Coventry and the constable are here and have a few more questions for you."

"About Lily," she whispered.

"Aye. Come now," he urged. He slid his arm around her waist and led her to the sitting room.

The constable was the first to speak. "Mrs. Broadbank, thank you for agreeing to speak with me. I'll keep my questions to a minimum."

"See that you do, constable," Edmund warned. "My wife has had a shock and needs time to recover."

"Edmund, where's Lily?" she asked.

He pulled her closer to his side. "The physician is taking care of her."

"My sister doesn't need me anymore, does she?"

"No, love."

"She said adoption papers were in her reticule. When we asked her to sign them, I didn't realize we would put her life in danger."

"We found them. Honeywell was after more than your sister."

"Coin to line his pockets," she whispered.

"And Thorne House. Why don't you sit down by the fire?" He urged her into one of the worn, but serviceable wing-back chairs.

She grasped his hand. "Stay?"

"I won't leave you," he promised. He nodded to the constable and said, "Make it quick."

The constable had Addy tell him what happened—twice. When she'd repeated the same sequence of events, Edmund interrupted the questioning.

"She's answered your questions. You should be questioning the man who attempted to murder my wife. If not for my sister-in-law selflessly giving her life, he would have succeeded."

He swept Addy into his arms and stalked from the room. Mr. Wythe was waiting at attention, his eyes filled with pain. Edmund knew the retainer felt responsible, though there was nothing he could have done to stop the determined man who had followed Lily to their sanctuary.

The man's voice broke as he advised, "The physician is waiting to examine Addy."

Edmund and Addy followed Mr. Wythe up the stairs to the bedchamber he and his wife shared.

"Mr. Broadbank," the physician intoned as they entered the room. "If you would summon Mrs. Wythe, I will call you—"

"I am not leaving my wife's side."

The physician nodded. "Very well. Would you rather sit or lie down, Mrs. Broadbank?"

"Sit, thank you," Addy replied.

The physician gently took Addy's face in his hands and looked into her eyes, all the while asking how she felt, what she had for breakfast, and how old their son was.

"Oh, he's not our son yet," she told the physician. "He will be once we adopt him."

"Who is his mother?"

Addy's eyes filled as she whispered, "An angel."

His gaze met Edmund's who repeated what Addy had told him an hour earlier, "Her sister signed the adoption papers and told Addy that she was Adam's mum now."

"Who is the angel?"

Addy's tears slowly fell. "Lily. My sister promised she would be Adam's angel."

"Mrs. Broadbank, I'm going to prescribe a hot bath." The doctor turned to Edmund. "The hotter the better, with lavender…it has soothing qualities."

Edmund frowned. "Is that all?"

"Laudanum if she becomes agitated."

"No laudanum," Addy told them. "I need to be awake and aware if

Adam needs me during the night. He may have bad dreams."

"I shall leave the laudanum with the dosage in case you change your mind. If you prefer a bit of brandy."

Addy shuddered. "Vile stuff."

"Is there another type of spirits you would prefer?"

"A small glass of Mrs. Wythe's medicinal Irish whiskey," she replied. "She keeps it in the pantry."

The physician rose to his feet. "Whiskey it is. Try to rest after your bath, Mrs. Broadbank."

"I will—thank you, doctor."

Edmund walked him to the door. "I shall be right outside, Addy."

"Do not attempt to put laudanum in my tea, Edmund."

He swallowed the need to laugh at her irate tone. "I won't." Once they were in the hallway, he asked, "How long will it take for her to recover from the shock?"

"Your wife seems to be a strong-minded woman," the physician replied.

Edmund scrubbed a hand over his face. "You have no idea."

"With rest, and an invalid's diet, she should be able to resume her normal duties in a few days. Though the mind heals in its own time. I cannot say for certain, but because your son will need the both of you while he gets over his fear of hearing—though not seeing—what occurred, he too will need to be as quiet as possible, with a bland diet."

Edmund mumbled, "Good luck with that."

"Do the best you can. However, if he is an active child, let him return to his activities when he wants to. He may sleep more soundly for it."

"Thank you, doctor."

"Please do not hesitate to send for me—at any hour." With a glance over his shoulder at the open door, the doctor added, "The coroner should be arriving shortly. Please ensure that no one but the guard you have posted is with Miss Lovecote."

"You have my word."

As the physician descended the stairs, Edmund said a prayer for Lily and another for Adam and Addy before returning to her side.

"Now then, shall I ring for your bathwater?" he said.

"Will you stay with me?" Addy asked.

He strode to the bellpull in the corner of the room and gave it a sharp tug. "Of course." He pulled her to her feet, sat down, and gently tugged her onto his lap. When the footman arrived, he made his request. When they were alone once more, he asked, "Now then, my love, would you like me to scrub your back?"

She turned her face into his neck and sighed. "That sounds wonderful."

The weight of responsibility nearly crushed him. It was his fault that he'd been distracted by Honeywell's diversion of a messenger. "I wish I had not left you and Adam alone."

"You did not know it was part of that madman's plan."

Her words added to the weight on his shoulders. "I should have suspected it."

She stiffened in his arms. "Can we speak of something else?"

"What would you like to talk about, my love?"

"Mayhap I can scrub your back, too."

He remembered the delightful bath they'd shared the first night they arrived. The tub was large enough for two—and for the lovemaking that interrupted their bathing. Mayhap he could make her forget the horror of the afternoon, if only for a little while.

He lowered his lips and gently brushed them against hers. "I think I can be persuaded to join you—on one condition."

"Oh, what is that?"

"That you don't get soap in my eyes again."

Her soft chuckle was music to his ears. "I won't." There was a brief pause before she said, "Edmund?"

"Yes, love?"

"Did you know the moment you walked into Mrs. Dove-Lyon's private office, I was captivated by you?"

He chuckled. "Would that have been the bruises on my face or the swelling?"

She held his gaze, her eyes swirling with a mix of emotions—sorrow...worry...and love. "I saw past the minor swelling and the bruises."

"Did you?"

She pressed a kiss to the base of his jaw. "Mmm. It was your stormy gray eyes and broad shoulders that nearly stole my breath."

"Really? Tell me more."

She surprised him by asking, "What did you think when we first met?"

He pressed a kiss to her forehead, the end of her nose, and her upturned lips. "That I'd met a landlocked siren who'd simply stolen my heart."

"I love you, Edmund."

He captured her lips in a drugging kiss. Resting his forehead on hers, he professed, "I love you more."

Chapter Twenty-Five

Edmund stalked toward the entryway, demanding, "What is the meaning of this, Wythe? I gave strict instructions that my wife and son were not to be disturbed."

"I am *not* a disturbance!" replied Earl Templeton.

"Father?"

"Why did you not tell me you'd married? You have a son? Have you led a dual life, one that you kept secret from me?"

"Lower your voice. I'm beginning to see that Colin's similar affliction is not due solely to his time as a captain in the Royal Navy."

"I do not speak loudly," his father replied.

"Edmund."

The soft voice of his wife had Edmund glancing over his shoulder. "Addy—I thought you were resting."

"I thought it best to see if I could calm whatever is happening. Adam needs his sleep."

"Adam?" The earl's eyes widened. "You're that actress!"

"You will not raise your voice in my home." Edmund glared at his father. "And you will never raise your voice to my wife or our son."

His father's eyes narrowed. "How old is your son?" Edmund stared at his father without responding until the earl sighed audibly. "Forgive me for intruding and possibly speaking louder than I intended."

ADDY TOOK A moment to see the worry in the depths of the earl's gaze. Had he heard about the attempt on her life—and the murder of her sister? The earl must have come to demand answers, though he had no right to any. The pain and sorrow in the depths of his gray eyes mirrored Edmund's.

"Mr. Wythe, would you please ask Mrs. Wythe to bring us tea—and something sweet—in the sitting room." She smiled at the earl. He was her father-in-law, though he had only just realized it. It would be up to her to soothe ruffled feathers. "Earl Templeton, welcome to our home. Our sitting room is lovely this time of day. The windows face the garden, although at this time of year, everything has finished blooming. Won't you join us for tea?"

The man's face flushed. She'd hoped if she ignored the way he'd addressed her in her own home and treated him with kindness that he would see how ungracious he had been. When he continued to stand there, confusion and embarrassment in his eyes, she glanced at her husband, who frowned, but inclined his head.

Edmund moved to stand beside her—protecting her, though she did not need it. "Father, allow Wythe to relieve you of your greatcoat, hat, and gloves."

Their retainer stepped forward to do so. The silence was a bit off-putting, and Addy knew her husband would not rush to forgive his father for his treatment of her. It would be up to her to mend the breach.

She beamed at the earl. "This way." Then she tugged on her husband's arm, leaned close, and whispered, "Be nice!"

Edmund surprised her by giving his father a brief tour as they walked along the hallway. One of the footmen moved past them to open the sitting room doors. Her husband inclined his head. "Thank you."

The earl had been silent while Edmund expounded on the history of her grandmother's home. It warmed her heart that her husband had listened and remembered when she'd spoken of Thorne House on their journey here.

"The room is most pleasant," the older man acknowledged. "Moreland Chase has a sitting room that my wife preferred above all others. It faced her gardens…" He trailed off as he turned to face his son. "It has been too long since I've remembered how much your mother loved spending time in the sunlight—inside her sitting room and outside in her gardens."

Edmund's expression softened. "She scolded me more than once when I pricked my fingers trying to pick roses for her."

Tea arrived, and Addy was grateful for the interruption.

"Shall I pour?" asked the housekeeper.

"No thank you, Mrs. Wythe," Addy replied. "Would you please ask Maisy to bring Adam as soon as he wakes from his nap?"

"Of course, Mrs. Broadbank."

Addy smiled. "I wouldn't want him to fuss unnecessarily."

The housekeeper left them to their tea.

Addy poured, serving the earl first. His brow furrowed as he accepted the cup. "Isn't Mrs. Wythe a bit old for the position of housekeeper?"

If the earl was going to be difficult, she would have to bend over backward to ensure she said nothing to antagonize him. "My grandmother hired them. They have been at Thorne House for forty years and are quite indispensable to me."

"To what do we owe the pleasure of your visit, Father?" Edmund interjected.

Addy was about to assure the earl he was welcome anytime when he responded, "I was at Templeton House recently, to congratulate Colin and Gemma on their news. Despite his not taking my advice, he managed to find the perfect wife."

"I cannot agree more. Gemma is kind, caring, and will be an excellent mother."

"When she mentioned *your* son, Colin immediately fell silent, refusing to answer my questions."

"So, you decided to hie off to Leeds to insult my wife with your insinuations?"

"Edmund, I'm certain that is not the case," Addy said. Gathering her courage, she set her teacup and saucer on the table between the settees and faced the earl. "To answer your earlier question, I am not that *actress*—but I am the one who traveled to Templeton House in search of the man my sister claimed was the father of the child she carried."

"I did not come here to listen to tall tales!" the earl thundered.

She lifted her chin and met the intensity of his glare. "That is a relief, because I do not have any tales to tell you. What I will share with you is the truth. My sister and Adam were in love, but something happened—I do not know what—and she left the stage and returned here during her confinement. When I asked if Adam knew about the babe, she admitted he did not."

"So, you took it upon yourself to find out?" The earl's speculative expression was much preferred to his accusatory one.

"Yes."

"Why?"

Uncertainty filled her. Should she answer the earl, or ignore his question. Edmund grasped her hand in the warmth of his. The connection between them was strong, his silent message received. Answer truthfully. His smile warmed her heart and gave her the strength to continue. "Earl Templeton, do you love your sons?"

"What kind of question is that?"

"An honest one, Father," Edmund said. "One I'd appreciate you answering."

The earl set down his cup and saucer. "Of course I love my sons—all of them."

"Then you can understand why I felt it my duty to let Adam know my sister carried his babe," Addy said. "Son or daughter, he had a right to know."

The earl stared at his hands. "And I treated you abominably."

When he raised his head, she noticed the bone-deep sorrow in his eyes. "I may not know what it is like to lose a son, and I hope I never do," she told him. "I do know what it is like to lose my parents to a freak accident…and my sister to a man who would kill for money."

Edmund was about to speak when they were interrupted by the knock on the door. "Come in." He rose to his feet and greeted their maid and son. "Ah, Maisy. Thank you for bringing Adam to meet his grandfather. Would you mind staying? Adam is more at ease these days when you and Addy are with him."

Before he could grasp Adam's hand, the little boy raced over to where the earl sat and stared at him. "Gran'fer?"

Tears welled in the earl's eyes, and Addy's heart went out to him. She knew he would see the family resemblance and have to accept it…as she hoped the man would accept his grandson.

"It's a pleasure to meet you, young man." He nodded to Edmund before telling the little boy, "You look just like your father. His name was Adam, too."

Adam noticed the slices of teacake and squealed, "Cake!" The tension in the room dissolved when he asked, "Please?"

"Someone with such excellent manners definitely deserves cake." The earl paused. "With your permission, Mrs. Broadbank."

"Please, call me Addy," she replied.

The earl inclined his head. "With your permission, Addy."

"He tends to make a bit of a mess when he eats."

Edmund chuckled. "He does everything with gusto, just like—"

"His father," the earl finished. "As I am traveling, I have a small trunk with a few changes of clothing. I don't mind crumbs."

"Adam, if you sit quietly next to your grandfather, you can have cake."

Before either of them could move, Adam climbed up onto the settee and sat with his hands in his lap.

"Serve the lad his cake," the earl directed. "May he have a cup of weak tea with it?"

"Milky tea," Adam corrected him. "Please, Gran'fer?"

As Addy served the requested tea, the earl surprised them by carrying on a mostly one-sided conversation with his grandson while he fed him bits of cake. Adam finished the cake and slurped the half cup of tea Addy had handed to him.

"You have crumbs on your chin, my love." Addy rose from her seat, but the earl waved at her to remain seated.

"Allow me. Master Adam, can you wipe your chin?"

The little boy managed to remove most of the crumbs and beamed at the earl. "All gone?"

"Good enough," the earl replied, then grunted in surprise when Adam climbed onto his lap and leaned against him. Shock and need swirled in the depths of the earl's eyes as he wrapped an arm around the little one.

"Would you like me to take him to the nursery, Mrs. Broadbank?" Maisy asked.

"If you wouldn't mind—"

"Nonsense," the earl interrupted. "My grandson and I need to inspect my horses to see that your stable master is taking proper care of them."

"Horsies!"

The earl laughed, a warm, deep laugh, so like Edmund's that Addy's heart warmed at the sound. The change that had come over the man from the moment Adam walked into the room with Maisy was such a relief.

"Care to join us, son?" the earl asked.

"What about Addy?" Edmund replied.

"You are more than welcome to join us, Addy. Though I thought we Broadbank men would get out of your hair for a little and give you a chance to rest. If Adam is anything like his father or uncles, even with Maisy's help, I know how exhausting it is caring for—and chasing after—my grandson."

Edmund rose and walked over to his father. "Thank you, Father." The earl raised one eyebrow in silent question, and Edmund chuckled. "For accepting my wife and son."

"Poppa! Gran'fer—horsies!" With Edmund holding one little hand and the earl holding the other, Adam smiled at Addy. "Bye, Mum!"

"Wait for Maisy to get your coat, Adam," she said.

When he pouted, the earl leaned down and told him, "Your father and I will be wearing our coats, too. Best to listen to your mother—she knows best."

Adam nodded and led his father and grandfather into the hallway to wait for Maisy.

Watching her men leave, Addy knew she had made the right decision last year. Though she never would have thought her sister would give Adam into her care, she suspected all along that Lily could not refuse the call of the stage. Wishing with all her heart that her sister had not sacrificed herself, Addy knew if their places had been reversed, she would have done the same for Lily.

"Ah, there you are, Mrs. Broadbank." Mrs. Wythe entered the sitting room. "Would you like to approve the luncheon and dinner menus?"

Addy laughed. "We normally don't bother with such. Did you

create one for our esteemed guest?"

"Of course. I cannot have the earl thinking my Addy is not capable of running Thorne House."

"Mrs. Wythe, you have always looked out for Lily and me, and now, Adam and Edmund. Have I thanked you yet today?"

"You did at breakfast. Now, why don't we see what Cook can whip up for luncheon? Those three are guaranteed to return with appetites."

Chapter Twenty-Six

Mrs. Wythe had been correct in her assumption. The trio had returned professing to be starving—well, at least Edmund and the earl had. Luncheon was a merry affair, even though Adam had eaten in the nursery with Maisy.

Over their cups of tea, the earl turned to Addy. "I feel I must apologize again, Addy. I can only assert that in my grief I was not willing to listen to anything that would question my son's good name."

Thinking of Lily and the two affairs she was aware of, Addy knew she would have done the same had someone called her sister's name into question. "I forgive you, and of course I understand, your lordship."

The earl's relief was evident. "I would prefer if you did not address me as your lordship."

Hurt lanced through Addy.

Edmund rose to his feet, and the earl waved at him to sit down. "I would much prefer if you called me Father."

"Thank you, Father," she rasped. "I would be honored."

"Excellent. Now, when can I expect to meet my next grandson?" Edmund snorted with laughter, and his father joined in. "Too intrusive a question, I know, but I'm not getting any younger."

"I daresay Colin and Gemma will be providing you with a grandson or granddaughter by late spring—mayhap sooner," Edmund said.

The earl set his teacup carefully on its saucer. "And I look forward to that blessed event, but I'm not solely thinking of myself. Adam needs a brother—or sister to look after. You, Colin, and Adam had one another to play with and get in trouble with. Though Adam's gone"—the earl's voice broke—"Master Adam is a reminder of that joyous time in my life. Now then, I believe Edmund is expecting guests. Shall I take myself off?"

Addy frowned at her husband, then turned back to the earl. "We would love to have you stay with us for a few days, Father. Although I am not certain whom my husband is expecting. It is not like him not to inform me of such things."

The earl chuckled. "A messenger arrived while we were in the stables. I trust he will explain it all to you when the time comes. It appears to be of some urgency, that he meet with these men."

"Captain Coventry and Mr. King are coming?" she asked.

"Aye, Addy," Edmund replied. "I did not want to worry you unnecessarily."

"Having them arrive without my knowledge is even more worrying, Edmund."

"Give the lad the benefit of the doubt," the earl said. "He was protecting you and my grandson."

Addy acquiesced. "I do not have to like it but will concede that he does deserve the benefit of the doubt." She rose from her seat, and the men immediately followed. "If you will excuse me, I shall speak to our cook to ensure she has enough prepared for unexpected visitors and teatime." She smiled at the earl. "Please do stay with us."

He returned her smile and bowed. "I should be delighted. Thank you, Addy."

WHEN SHE LEFT the room, the earl demanded. "Tell me what has happened and leave nothing out!"

Edmund related the rumors and the blackmail attempt.

"Colin did not inform me of this!"

"Given your heated reaction just now, can you blame him?" Edmund asked. "Gemma is expecting and should not have to be subjected to two Broadbank men bellowing."

His father's mouth hung open for a moment before he harrumphed. "I do not bellow."

Edmund chuckled. "Indeed, Father. You pronounce, proclaim, and demand at a volume above what is considered polite...but you do *not* bellow."

"Exactly. Now then, tell me the rest."

As directed, Edmund shared the information Coventry and King had gathered and informed him of the number of guards currently situated in and around Templeton House, Thorne House...and Moreland Chase.

The shock was expected, but the rasped reply was not. "Did your contact feel guards at Moreland Chase were warranted?"

"Aye, Father. Honeywell has a number of contacts in London's stews and gaming hells. Colin and I felt it best to have them in place and explain it to you later—"

"If I discovered they were there," the earl finished.

"We would protect you as you have protected us over the years."

"I have been blessed with three wonderful sons who have grown into men I am immensely proud of. You have both married women suited to you. I could not ask for more."

"Except for more grandchildren."

The earl laughed heartily. "Aye. I promise to pester you until you present me with another grandson...or granddaughter."

Edmund was still laughing when Mr. Wythe announced the arrival of Coventry and King.

"Show them into the library, would you, Wythe?"

"Of course, sir," the butler replied.

"After you, Father."

They were soon joined by Captain Coventry and Gavin King of the Bow Street Runners.

"Earl Templeton," Coventry said, "it's a pleasure to see you again."

"And you, captain." The earl nodded to King. "Are you here to impart distressing or bad news?"

"Neither," King informed him.

"I see—do you need to speak to my son privately?"

"Not at all, your lordship," King assured him.

"Please have a seat, gentlemen," Edmund offered. "Have there been any further developments?"

"Honeywell is being held at Newgate," King replied.

Edmund nodded. "He should pay for his crimes."

"The charge of murder is a serious one," Coventry added. "That the target was the daughter-in-law of Earl Templeton adds to the weight of the charge."

Edmund exchanged glances with his father. "I'm sensing hesitance on your part, Coventry."

"As the victim was Addy's sister—" Coventry began.

The earl interrupted, "The charge will not carry the same weight." He held up his hand. "Before you say anything, please know I do not hold to such thinking. A life has been ended, most brutally. Honeywell should pay the price. Has anyone stepped forward to speak on his behalf?"

"Not as yet, though there are rumors," Coventry replied.

"Will my input see that the man will hang for the murder of Miss Lily Lovecote?"

"Though it would help, I do not see that it will change the outcome should more than one peer speak on Honeywell's behalf."

"The man murdered the mother of my grandson—Adam's son is the heir to the viscountcy."

"Are you prepared to announce that publicly?" King asked. "It could have a devastating effect on Master Adam and Mrs. Broadbank."

Edmund added, "My wife should be a part of this conversation."

"Agreed," the earl said as he strode over to the bellpull and tugged on it. Mr. Wythe arrived a few moments later. "Please ask my daughter-in-law to join us." Mr. Wythe left to do his bidding, and the earl turned to his son. "Forgive me for speaking out of turn. I tend to forget myself and take charge when serious matters are affecting my family."

"Nothing to forgive, Father."

A FEW MOMENTS later, Addy arrived. "You wished to see me?"

Edmund walked over to her and placed his arm around her waist. "King and Coventry have brought the news that Honeywell is currently at Newgate."

"I take it there is more, or you would not have summoned me."

"Yes, my love." He turned to the earl. "Father, would you care to explain the circumstances, or shall I?"

"You should," his father replied. "Addy loves you and trusts you to tell her the truth."

Edmund wished he could erase the fear that lingered in the blue-green depths of his wife's eyes, but now he was about to add to it.

"Father has suggested that in order for Honeywell to pay for murdering Lily, he would need to announce that she was Adam's mother and that my brother was his father."

She frowned, digesting his words. "The fact that she was murdered is not enough," she rasped. "Is it?"

"If more than one peer steps forward to speak on Honeywell's behalf," the earl replied, "he may go free."

Her stomach ached at the thought that the man who'd brutally murdered her sister would go free. Lily was dead, and Addy knew she had to protect the living—Adam's family.

She leaned against her husband and met the earl's direct gaze. "Though you may not agree with me, we must protect the living, Father. We must protect your family—yourself, Colin and Gemma, Edmund and Adam. The earldom and the viscountcy must also be protected for future generations." Edmund pressed a kiss to the top of her head, giving her the courage to continue. "My sister will always be important to me. Edmund and I have agreed that Adam will need to know his birth parents as well as his adopted ones. In my heart I believe we should let the dead rest easy, knowing that their love will live on in Adam, while Edmund and I will do all in our power to protect Adam and your family."

"And if Colin and Gemma have a son?" the earl asked. "How do you propose to ensure Adam inherits the title?"

"That would never be my decision to make, Father. It is Colin and Gemma's decision."

"I had entertained thoughts of guiding you in your marriage decision, Edmund, especially since I did not have the opportunity to do so with either of your brothers. I must tell you, I believe you have found the perfect wife." The earl extended his hand to Addy. Grasping hers, he said, "My dear, I am proud to call you daughter. I am confident you and Edmund will raise Adam's son, and any other children God blesses you with, to know right from wrong and will have the same strong conviction to protect his family and our name at all costs."

Addy was not aware that she was weeping until her father-in-law handed her his handkerchief.

Flustered by her tears, the earl asked, "Has my daughter been weepy as of late, Edmund?"

"What with all that has occurred, can you blame her?" Edmund replied.

The earl smiled, knowingly. "Not at all. Though I would, however, place the blame firmly on your shoulders."

Edmund tensed, and Addy knew now was the perfect time to announce something. "I have good news, Edmund."

He loosened his hold on her and stared into her eyes. "Good news?"

"You're going to be a father."

Edmund wavered on his feet, but quickly righted himself as his father slapped him on the back. "Congratulations, son!" The earl then surprised Addy by embracing her and brushing a kiss to her cheek. "Do not overdo it, Addy." Turning to his son, he warned, "See that she rests and eats properly, or you shall answer to me!"

Edmund chuckled. "You have my word, Father."

Coventry and King added their congratulations before taking their leave, promising to keep the earl and the couple informed.

When it was just the three of them once more, the earl pulled her into his embrace. "How soon will Adam wake from his nap?"

Epilogue

Nine months later...

Edmund held Adam's hand as they approached the bed and leaned down to whisper, "Remember to keep your voice low so you do not wake your little brother."

"I will, Poppa."

"There you are." Addy smiled as Adam carefully climbed on the bed and snuggled on one side of her, staring at the babe in her arms. "You are a big brother now, Adam. You will have to watch over your little brother."

"I already promised Poppa." He used the tip of his finger to touch the tiny hand that flailed as the babe began to fuss.

Addy soothed him as she wrapped her arm around her son. "Would you like to stay awhile and keep us company?"

"What's his name, Mum?"

"Edmund."

"Like I'm Adam for my father?"

"Yes, my love."

Adam scrambled off the bed. "Poppa, I need a sister."

Edmund gaped at their son. "Your mum just gave you a little brother. We need to let her rest."

"You can call her Lily, after my mother."

Edmund squatted down in front of Adam. "You are absolutely right, but these things take time. Why don't you kiss your mum, and we'll ask Giles to take you to your grandfather. He said something about going to the stables."

Adam did as he was bade and pressed a quick kiss on Addy's cheek. Edmund went with him to speak to the footman.

When Edmund returned to her side and sat, she lifted a hand to his face. "I was blessed the day Mrs. Dove-Lyon arranged our lives without our knowing it."

"She does have a way of looking below the surface to the heart of the matter." Edmund placed the tip of his finger beneath her chin, tilting her face up. "How are you feeling, my love?"

Addy smiled. "Blessed…exhilarated…loved."

He pressed his lips to hers. "My brave love. You aren't tired and sore?"

"Mayhap a bit," she admitted. "Why don't you kiss me again and remind me what we have missed while our son was getting ready to make his presence known?"

Edmund drew sustenance from her lips, deepening the kiss as a reminder and a promise of the nights they would share once she recovered from the birthing.

Brushing the tips of his fingers along the curve of her cheek, the line of her jaw, he rasped, "I love you, Addy."

"I love you more."

About the Author

Historical & Contemporary Romance "Warm…Charming…Fun…"

C.H. was born in Aiken, South Carolina, but her parents moved back to northern New Jersey where she grew up.

She believes in fate, destiny, and love at first sight. C.H. fell in love at first sight when she was seventeen. She was married for 41 wonderful years until her husband lost his battle with cancer. Soul mates, their hearts will be joined forever.

They have three grown children—one son-in-law, two grandsons, two rescue dogs, and two rescue grand-cats.

Her characters rarely follow the synopsis she outlines for them…but C.H. has learned to listen to her characters! Her heroes always have a few of her husband's best qualities: his honesty, his integrity, his compassion for those in need, and his killer broad shoulders. C.H. writes about the things she loves most: Family, her Irish and English Ancestry, Baking and Gardening.

Sláinte!
C.H.

C.H.'s Social Media Links:
Website: www.chadmirand.com
Amazon: amazon.com/stores/C.-H.-Admirand/author/B001JPBUMC
BookBub: bookbub.com/authors/c-h-admirand
Facebook Author Page: facebook.com/CHAdmirandAuthor
Facebook Private Reader's Page ~ C.H. Reader's Nook:
facebook.com/groups/714796299746980
GoodReads: goodreads.com/author/show/212657.C_H_Admirand
Instagram: c.h.admirand
Twitter: @AdmirandH
Youtube: youtube.com/channel/UCRSXBeqEY52VV3mHdtg5fXw

Made in United States
Troutdale, OR
06/26/2024